"Who the devil are you?"

Camilla's eyes flew open to stare at the man standing over her.

"If you're aiming on hitching a ride out to the Cay, forget it. I don't run a free taxi service."

Cam struggled for composure. "I was told to wait here. My name is Camilla Lucas."

"Camilla Lucas," he repeated, his disbelief apparent. With a sudden movement he tweaked off her large heavy-framed sunglasses. He shook his head. "But surely, Miss Camilla Lucas is a prim little old lady complete with thimble, needle and thread."

"I'm very sorry to disappoint you," she said, a shade waspishly, nervousness icing her voice.

His eyes flickered over her again in a deliberate provocative inspection. "Oh, you don't, my dear Miss Camilla Lucas. Not at all."

RACHEL FORD was born in Coventry, descended from a long line of Warwickshire farmers. She met her husband at Birmingham University, and he is now a principal lecturer in a polytechnic school. Rachel and her husband both taught school in the West Indies for several years after their marriage and have had fabulous holidays in Mexico, as well as unusual experiences in Venezuela and Ecuador during revolutions and coups! Their two daughters were born in England. After stints as a teacher and information guide, Rachel took up writing, which she really enjoys doing the most—first children's and girls' stories, and finally romance novels.

Books by Rachel Ford

HARLEQUIN PRESENTS
1160—A SHADOWED LOVE
1304—LOVE'S FUGITIVE

HARLEQUIN ROMANCE
2913—CLOUDED PARADISE

RACHEL FORD

web of desire

Harlequin Books

TORONTO • NEW YORK • LONDON
AMSTERDAM • PARIS • SYDNEY • HAMBURG
STOCKHOLM • ATHENS • TOKYO • MILAN

Harlequin Presents first edition February 1991
ISBN 0-373-11337-4

Original hardcover edition published in 1989
by Mills & Boon Limited

WEB OF DESIRE

CHAPTER ONE

THE WHITE louvre windows were stiff with disuse. They yielded only reluctantly to the man's hand, as he moved down the length of the enormous room, gradually releasing a waterfall of dazzling tropical light and heat into the fetid greenish darkness. When he had opened the final shutter he stood, his eyes travelling almost disbelievingly across the four huge tapestries that lined one wall.

Then he moved slowly across to the nearest one and gently, almost reverently, lifted a corner of the heavy cloth . . . Not bad condition, really, considering they were all of three hundred years old . . . All the same, though, they'd need some sort of expert to get them back to their original glory . . . He'd have one sent down from the States right away. Hold on, though—the tapestries were from England, weren't they? At least, that was the old story. Well, he'd send for an English restorer, then, and preferably—a fleeting smile temporarily softened the lines of his austere face as his gaze moved once more along the scenes depicted in the woven panels—one who was extremely broad-minded.

Aloud, he said decisively into the silent room, 'I'll write today.'

'But, Camilla, darling,' the flimsy airmail letter fluttered to the dining-table from Celia Lucas's hands as she fixed her china-blue eyes on her daughter, 'you can't possibly want to go to Tamarind. Think how it would hurt me to know that you were there in my old home. And as for that man, Matthew Corrigan——' Her small, neat face tightened and she almost spat out the name.

Cam sighed inwardly. Ever since the letter had arrived on her desk in the museum that morning, together with the typcially laconic note from the Keeper of Textiles—'Interested? Could be useful experience. Think I can fix your secondment with the director'—she had known how her mother would react. And it was perfectly understandable that she should feel this way. But, none the less, it was far too exciting an opportunity—in so many ways—for her to turn it down.

'He cheated us—cheated me!' Her mother's voice rose. 'He's nothing but a common thief. I was only a child, but I knew what his game was. Coming to play cards with Father every evening, then that dreadful night persuading him into one final hand, after deliberately losing all the previous games. And setting those ridiculous stakes. Poor Father, he was so unwell.'

Unwell? So drunk, surely? Cam hastily turned her violet eyes downwards to her place-mat to hide the momentary flash of irritation which she was certain must be all too apparent. After all, if her grandfather had been a weak fool, then he had paid a hundred times for the luxury of that folly, before dying a ruined man when she herself had not even been born. In one rigged game of cards, on that torrid, tropical night, he had lost not only Tamarind, his beautiful home, but Halcyon Cay, the small Caribbean island on which it stood—everything.

And poor Mummy, Cam thought with a surge of pity, she had lost too. She had paid a thousand times over—and was still paying. She had gone to bed a rich, indulged girl, and woken a pauper's child. And

Matthew Corrigan . . . momentarily her eyes strayed with awful fascination to the sprawling signature in black ink across the bottom of the letter which lay open between them. For an instant, a strange, slightly unnerving shiver rippled across the soft skin on the nape of her neck. Those bold, arrogant strokes . . . If handwriting revealed personality, then here, surely, was a tough, uncompromising old man.

Other children had snuggled down with Snow White's wicked stepmother, the wolf in grandmother's bed; she, from before her earliest memories began, had had this ogre Matthew Corrigan for nightly company, so real that she had almost been able to conjure up the flush of sadistic triumph on his dark face as he stood at the foot of the wide sweep of staircase, looking down out of a pitiless face at her grandfather, who was slumped against the bottom stair, his eyes closed tightly against the spectre of what he had done. *What big teeth you have. All the better to eat you with, my dear.* Now, seeing that imperious, powerful signature, it was rather as though the ogre, a wolf's smile still on his face, had leapt straight on to the faded rug in front of the fireplace over there . . .

'Of course, it's for you I most regret it, darling.' Her mother sighed gently, and Cam roused herself from her none too pleasant daydream. 'You would be an heiress, Camilla Forrester Lucas of Tamarind House. I would have given a ball for you, and all the rich, eligible young men from the islands——'

'Oh, Mummy, please,' Cam cut through the plaintive wail. 'Don't upset yourself about it all over again.' She shot her mother a determinedly cheerful smile. 'You know I don't like dancing, and although I've never met a rich, eligible young man, I'm sure I wouldn't like him if I did.'

'But then you wouldn't have to work in that horrid, dirty old museum. You're a beauty—at least you would be, if you took the trouble to make more of yourself—and you should be surrounded by beautiful things.' Her mother's eyes flickered around the drab room. 'Not living like this——'

'Stop it, Mummy.' Cam shook her head, half laughing, half serious, then pushed a tendril of long, dark blonde hair back behind her ear. 'You know very well I love working in the museum, and after all, it was you who taught me to sew so well——'

'Yes, but I wanted you to do nice, pretty embroidery, like tray cloths and doilies, not be a career girl and shut yourself away in that nasty attic workroom of yours all day long. And for you to have to work on those tapestries! I was never allowed to see them, of course, but from what I heard . . . What your father would have said . . .'

Poor Daddy. A pang shot through Cam as she remembered the thin, permanently careworn-looking man who had died when she was ten. Looking back, she wondered for a moment whether his spirit had not been drained by the constant strain of coping with his wife's thwarted delusions of grandeur. But she pushed this disloyal thought from her. She, more than anyone, knew the sacrifices her mother had made for her—year after year of going without in this increasingly shabby house: no holidays; none of the pretty clothes which her mother's feminine nature craved, in order to achieve what to her mind were the right things for her only daughter. Music and deportment lessons, private schools, of course—though Cam herself, walking home in boater and grey serge blazer, had often looked with secret envy at the children from their local comprehensive school, who had always seemed, at least to her, so much more carefree and fun-loving. It was for this same reason of gratitude—tinged on occasion with guilt—that she bore with such patient good humour the smothering, over-protective relationship that her mother had imposed on her.

'And besides, you're nearly twenty-five. How will you ever find a husband?'

'But I don't want one.' Cam sliced a chunk of tinned pineapple into two neat halves with her spoon. 'I love my job in that nasty attic far too much. I forgot to tell you—we've been given a pair of old Spanish prie-dieu chairs, and I've nearly finished restoring the seat tapestries. They were in a terrible state, but when I've done the repairs they'll look wonderful.' Her small, delicate face glowed. 'And as for this house, well, it's always been my home and I love it. You were saying we must have this room and the hall done up——'

'Not before time, and your bedroom . . .'

'Well, he—Mr Corrigan—is offering very generous payment.' Momentarily, her eyes widened at the memory of the sum offered to cover her expenses.

Her mother sniffed. 'He can afford it, on our money——'

'And with my salary as well, we'll be able to have it all done when I get back. So I can't possibly not go.' She gave her mother a teasing smile. 'Besides, it's your fault if I want to see Tamarind. You've told me so much about the wonderful life you all had out there, and I'd love to see it just once. And Mr Corrigan hasn't the faintest idea who I am—after all, who's going to associate Camilla Lucas from London with the Forresters of Tamarind?' She began gathering the dishes together. 'You won't be lonely. Now Mrs Stuart is back from her winter cruise, you can start your bridge parties again. And although the director says he'll

arrange secondment for up to three months, I'm sure
I'll only be away a few weeks.'

The hundred-decibel cricket commentary from the cab
driver's radio debarred any conversation between St
Hilaire airport and the town. Cam was grateful, though.
She leaned forward in the rear seat of the ageing Buick,
her blonde hair blown back from her hot face by the
purely artificial breeze created by their literally hair-
raising speed, and stared out incredulously.

Nothing, she thought dazedly, not her mother's
endless descriptions, not television films, not the
guidebooks to the West Indies which she had skimmed
through in the previous couple of weeks, nothing had
prepared her for this—this almost physical assault on
her senses of heat and colour, vivid, exciting—almost
frightening. Everywhere was lush growth: a riot of
bougainvillaea, crimson, purple and apricot sprawling
over every whitewashed wall . . . huge trees covered with
a scarlet lacework of flowers. To one side of the dusty
road, the turquoise sea sparkled with tiny points of
light; to the other, the ground rose sharply towards the
blue hills, skirted by a tangle of creeper-festooned
shrubs.

She sank back into the sagging upholstery, her mind
filled with a strange sensation, a sort of childish pre-
Christmas mixture of excitement, exultation and, at the
same time, apprehension. Strange that Mummy hadn't
told her about all this. Most of her endless talk of
life at Tamarind had been about beach parties, afternoon calls, invitations to St Hilaire to the Governor-
General's annual garden party, servants who came in
response to a single handclap . . .

The road curved between tall, arching bamboos and,
momentarily, under their rustling coolness, she lost

sight of the sea and the hills. Then they were into the outskirts of the capital, Port Charlotte, driving past neat duplex bungalows, through the small town centre with its tiny square and Victorian-style fountain, all of which had a kind of run-down raffish elegance, and finally to the waterfront and wharf, where a thin file of men were loading huge stems of green bananas on to a rusty-looking cargo boat.

At the far end of the stone quay, a large, rapacious-looking power-boat was tied up. The Buick skidded to a halt alongside, the driver leapt from his seat, lifted out her cases and courteously, though absent-mindedly, deposited her and them on the edge of the quay. Cam began fumbling uncertainly for her purse, but he waved it away.

'He's paid already.'

'He?'

Her query went unanswered, though, for from the radio the applause crackled across the Atlantic at yet another West Indian boundary stroke, and the driver scrambled back in. She put a restraining hand on the side of the car.

'But—but what am I to do?'

'He say you to wait.'

The driver grinned broadly up at her, then shot off with a lazily friendly wave, the sounds receding with him, so that she was left standing quite alone on the deserted quay, with only the gentle slap of water at her feet.

A vague sense of grievance began needling her, and she tapped one high-heeled toe impatiently. No doubt old Mr Corrigan had sent one of his servants across from Halcyon Cay to pick her up, and he had taken the chance to skip off on his own account. 'You'll have to watch the servants, darling. They get away with anything they can.' A faint frown creased Cam's delicate brow. Her mother's warning was obviously well-founded.

In the meantime, though, she was beginning to feel decidedly uncomfortable. Her neat beige jersey suit, which back in England had seemed ideal for travel, was now sticking to her, as were her tights, so that her whole body was wrapped in an unpleasant clamminess. Her head and neck were burning under the broiling afternoon sun, but when she looked around her there was no shelter of any description from the intense glare. She dug out from her bag a large cream cotton headscarf, draping it to cover as much of her head and shoulders as she could, then stood disconsolately, first on one foot, then the other, to try to ease the nagging ache in her ankles.

Across the waterfront, the men had finished loading the bananas. They came down the gangplank, eyeing her curiously, and drifted away in twos and threes, their shouted conversations echoing over the oily water and making her feel even more isolated and conspicuous. She looked anxiously down the length of the quay, but no one was bustling towards her, full of apologies.

Oh, this was utterly ridiculous! On a sudden angry impulse, she snatched up her two cases, then the large vinyl grip with her tapestry restoration kit, lowered them into the well of the power-boat and then scrambled in beside them. There was no cabin; apart from the small deck area, the enormous engine obviously took up all the rest of the space. Still, there was at least a narrow slatted bench at the rear, and she sank down on to it gratefully.

With her elbows leaning on the highly polished rail, she let her eyes travel slowly past the run-down waterfront buildings, across the murky harbour water, to the blue-green open sea where little boats were skimming. There was something hypnotically soothing about those tiny, white-sailed toy boats. She yawned and, resting her chin on her arms, closed her eyes against the brilliance . . .

'Who the devil are you?'

There was a black shadow across her face, blotting out the sun, and when her eyes flew open a man was standing over her, dark and menacing against the brightness of the sky. She stared up at him, her mind still fuzzed by sleep.

'I—I'm——'

'If you're aiming on hitching a ride out to the Cay, you can forget it. I don't run a free taxi service.'

Cam struggled for composure. 'I—I was told to wait here. My name's Camilla Lucas.'

'Camilla Lucas?' he repeated, the disbelief patent in his voice. With a sudden movement, so quick that she could not jerk back, he reached forward and tweaked off her large, heavy-framed sunglasses, then placed one thumb in the loose knot of her headscarf, dragging it from her so that her hair, freed from its tidy, businesslike pleat, tumbled on to her shoulders in golden disarray.

As she gazed up at him, in mingled anger and apprehension, he stared at her, his eyes narrowing to take in her flushed face and body in one swift, all-encompassing glance, which was hardly less of a physical assault on her person than the lush beauty of the island had been on her senses a little while before.

'Extraordinary.' He shook his head. 'I don't believe it.'

'You'll have to watch the servants, darling . . .' And yet, for this man, even though—her eyes strayed momentarily, then hastily reverted to a position just to the right of his cold grey eyes—even though he was dressed only in faded denims, sleeveless black vest and canvas espadrilles, the lowly position of servant appeared somehow totally unfitting. Perhaps he was old Mr Corrigan's personal assistant—no, secretary, that was what they were called, wasn't it?

'Well, you'd better believe it,' she said, her nervous uncertainty injecting a freezing chill into her normally pleasant, rather soft voice. Nothing—the little private school which her mother had skimped to send her to, the quietly subdued embroidery and textiles department of her art college, that dingy attic at the museum, which all at once she felt a desperate yearning to be safely back in—nothing had equipped her to deal with a situation—or a man like this.

'But surely Miss Camilla Lucas is a prim little old lady, complete with thimble, needle and thread?' There was now an unnerving gleam of devilment in his eyes.

'I'm very sorry to disappoint you,' she said, a shade waspishly.

His eyes flickered over her again in a deliberate, provocative inspection. 'Oh, you don't, my dear Miss Camilla Lucas. Not at all.'

There was an insolent drawl in his voice which grated sourly on her. She simply would not allow herself to become any further embroiled in a sparring match with him, which in any case she knew she would undoubtedly lose, so she looked down ostentatiously at her wristwatch.

'Shouldn't we be going? Mr Corrigan is expecting me—I'm supposed to be there in time for dinner and I don't want to be late. Besides,' her tone took on a certain *hauteur*, 'I'm very anxious to see the tapestries for the first time—and preferably,' she added meaningfully, 'in daylight.'

The man slanted her a look from beneath dark, level brows. 'Oh, I'm so sorry. I do apologise,' he said, in a tone which was not in the least an apology. 'Of course, we mustn't keep Mr Corrigan waiting, must we?'

He swung round, lifted a large cardboard box, from which came the gentle clink of bottles, down from the quay and set it on the deck barely an inch from her toes. She noticed that he was moving with a slight awkwardness, and when he turned away to the controls the awkwardness became a pronounced limp.

Cam replaced her sunglasses and, from the safety of her dark lenses, surveyed him. Probably a sports injury, for with a physique like that—tall, lithely built, yet with a suggestion of innate power and strength in his back muscles and the breadth of his shoulders—he surely had to be an athlete . . . Her eyes travelled up to his dark brown hair, thick and springing into unruly little half-curls on his nape, where it was a shade overlong. His hands, resting negligently on the tiller now, as he gently eased the big boat out through the harbour, were surely more of an artist's hands though, slender and long-fingered, but with that same hint of inner strength . . .

Who was this man? American, from his accent, although, with his thin, rather hawkish face, high cheekbones and the straight, arrogant set of his nose, he was far removed from the crew-cut, amiable young American students whom she had encountered on the rare occasions when she'd emerged from her private sanctum into the public part of the museum. In fact, to her admittedly inexperienced eye, he seemed much closer to her image of a Latin-American—Mexican, perhaps . . .

Who was he? Personal assistant . . . sportsman . . . artist? Whatever he was, she thought with a sudden frisson of fear, there was a hint of cruelty in the hard lines of that profile—an intimidating, ruthless certainty that he would achieve what he wanted, regardless of what—or who—stood in his way . . . Those grey eyes, which against the tanned skin stood out with a light intensity . . . that thin mouth . . . A strange, disturbing sensation leapt through her. She had never, she was quite positive, set eyes on this man before, and yet—in spite of the intense heat, goose-pimples prickled uneasily all over her arms—he was somehow frighteningly familiar . . . As she studied his profile with a new, feverish intensity, those thin lips twitched almost imperceptibly and she realised that he was clearly all too aware of her silent scrutiny. Her cheeks scarlet, she turned her head away sharply, to concentrate on subduing her flurried breathing to normal again.

They were through the harbour entrance now. He opened the throttle and, almost as though the boat scented open water, the soft, pulsing purr beneath her feet changed, in a crescendo of noise, to a throbbing roar. As the prow met the first slapping waves, the boat rocked slightly then leapt forward under his hands, so that her shoulder was thrown into painful contact with the rail.

The speed and the wind on her face were engendering in her a bubbling exhilaration, so that she could have laughed out loud—a sensation so totally alien to her that it was faintly alarming. She lifted the headscarf, which had dropped into her lap, to curb her hair, which was being whipped around her face in a golden cloud, but then let it fall back into her lap.

There was a V-shaped white wake behind them, while ahead lay the open sea, turquoise, sapphire, aquamarine; an infinity of shades, all stretching to that silver point where the sea melted into the sky, and surely—her heart bounded under her ribs—there was a small, uncertain smudge, not of cloud but of land. It could have been any island, but as she stared at it with a suffocating intensity she knew by some deep instinct that it was Halcyon Cay. Her home—or rather, what should have been her home.

For a moment, a terrible desolation took hold of her. That they should have lost all this! A small flicker of anger ignited to flame inside her against the old man who now sat, like some gigantic spider, awaiting her arrival. But it was simply no use. She must put this anger from her, and do the job she had been hired to do, to the very best of her ability, as though they had been *any* tapestries, *any* house, *any* island . . .

They were passing a small dug-out fishing-boat, its nets trailing alongside. There was a shout and a wave, and the man waved back, yelled something quite incomprehensible and grinned broadly. That sudden smile illuminated his thin, tanned face with a flash of strong, very white teeth. *All the better to eat you with, my dear*. Cam's violet eyes opened wide with shock. *He was the man*! He was the man from her dreams—the face which had haunted her childhood! She swallowed, fighting down her irrational fears. But it was ridiculous, totally impossible. He simply couldn't be. And yet—she felt the colour drain from her cheeks—there was, underneath all the impossibility, a shiver in her mind at the absolute certainty that this man and the house were somehow coming together—no, *fusing* together in her consciousness.

CHAPTER TWO

THE ISLAND was coming up on them rapidly, and to subdue the unnerving sensations that were gnawing away at her Cam fixed her eyes on it. Quite small, hardly more than five miles in length, she judged, the vegetation a lush green, except inland, where a string of oddly shaped, almost conical hills shimmered blue in the heat haze.

The man had not spoken to her since they had left Port Charlotte. Now, he turned briefly, pointed ahead and shouted something which was totally lost in the powerful roar of the engine but which she lipread as 'Halcyon Cay', so she nodded and smiled mechanically.

They were close enough now to see a few imposing-looking white houses dotted at select intervals among the greenery and, at the far end of the island from where they seemed to be heading, what looked like a village of low, single-storey huts, from several of which rose lazy drifts of chimney smoke.

They were right in now, past the narrow ribbon of pale creamy sand and running alongside what was obviously a small, private jetty, a gravelled road leading directly from it up to a large white house which was set two or three hundred yards back from the seafront and almost obscured by trees. The man cut the engine and, in a sudden silence, they floated in the last couple of yards to lie alongside the jetty.

Cam smoothed back her hair with unsteady hands, feeling the exhilaration of that twenty-minute journey still upon her, and when he turned to her, quite unable to prevent herself, she smiled up at him, wide-eyed.

'Oh, that was wonderful! The most marvellous trip I've——' she began; then, all at once conscious of the way his casual glance had deepened into intensity, she blushed in confusion and broke off.

He half raised one eyebrow in obvious amusement. 'I'm glad you enjoyed it. We try to give every—satisfacton to our visitors.'

At the unmistakable innuendo in his voice, the smile withered on her lips and picking up the abandoned headscarf, she arranged it deftly around her hairline, crossing the ends under her chin and knotting them behind, so that every windblown strand was securely out of sight.

He lifted the heavy box, swung it across to dump it, rather awkwardly, on the jetty, then turned back, steadying himself against the rail, and went to lift one of her cases. She sprang up.

'Oh, *please*, it's very heavy. Let me help.'

Unthinking, she put a hand on his wrist, but he shook it off impatiently.

'Thank you for your kind concern,' he said brusquely, 'but I just happen to have a bad leg. I'm not totally incapacitated.'

She sank back, her cheeks burning with mortification at this curt rebuff, and watched in silence as, with some difficulty, he hoisted off her other case and finally the vinyl zip bag which held all her equipment. He stretched a suntanned hand out to her but, still smarting, she ignored it, climbed up on to the bench seat, then, as the boat lurched, made an undignified scramble across to the jetty.

She stood without speaking as he began loading her cases into the back of a small, white, open runabout, but then, as he made to cavalierly toss her zip bag on top of the rest, she gasped urgently, 'Oh, please be careful. That has all my working gear in it.'

As he laid it down with exaggerated care, some imp of devilment impelled her to add, even while she was astonished at her own pertness, 'You know, my needle and thread—and my thimble, of course.'

He looked at her silently across the vehicle, a faint smile momentarily softening the bleakness of those grey eyes, then, motioning her into the runabout, swung himself in beside her and switched on the ignition.

His injured leg did not seem to inhibit his driving, she thought, as he took the vehicle from a standing start to fifty miles per hour in what seemed a split second, the gravel leaping beneath their wheels. And when they crossed the road to turn between two graceful white pillars into a wide driveway she could almost have sworn that they were travelling on two, not four wheels. Out here on Halcyon Cay the air was fresher and cooler than over on the oppressive mainland, but even so there was a damp perspiration on her brow and she clutched the side of the runabout with rigid, clammy hands.

The drive wound between an avenue of stately royal palms, and past them, when she plucked up the courage to open her eyes, she could see, fleetingly, undulating plantations of coconut palms and orange trees. And then, ahead of them suddenly on a little ridge was the house—Tamarind.

Welcome home, Miss Camilla. It's so good to have you here . . . Old family servants breaking down with tears of joy . . . Cam had fantasised for so long about this arrival that, now that the actual concrete moment was here, it bore a strange, almost light-headed quality of unreality. And besides, they were now racing up the drive at such a speed that she began to have a fatalistic feeling that she would never actually arrive; the open-topped vehicle was bucking so wildly that she clung desperately to the sides of her seat, fearing that she would be flung headlong out.

They rounded the last bend, scorched their way along the white façade and stopped so abruptly that she lunged helplessly sideways against the lean, hard body beside her before hurriedly straightening up again. It was the first time that their bodies had touched and, although the sensation was fleeting, the impact with that warm, solid frame left her face very flushed and her breathing fast and shallow.

She felt his eyes on her. 'Something wrong?' he asked casually.

Back in England, she had planned on savouring every precious second of this private, secret homecoming, but in the end she had been too intent on staying alive to give Tamarind more than the most cursory attention. He had spoiled it for her, and her fear crystallised into anger.

She leaned forward to retrieve her bag, which had been flung from her lap, and without turning, said, 'Tell me, are you always in quite such a hurry?'

There was more than a touch of asperity in her voice, but he merely replied offhandedly, 'Usually.' He gestured towards the house. 'If you ring the bell, someone will let you in. I'll take this lot round to the *servants'* entrance.'

His deliberately needling emphasis on the word discomfited her again, and she was almost positive that he was getting a great deal of private amusement at her expense. She got out slowly and stood watching as the runabout skidded round the corner in a flurry of grey dust. Only when it had disappeared did she turn slowly and survey the house.

She had grown up with the picture of this house imprinted on her mind, and yet somehow, in spite of her mother's frequent, yearning descriptions, she had not been prepared for the grandeur of Tamarind. Just beside her, a double-balustraded stone staircase led up to an enormous, white-pillared portico, to each side of which a wide veranda ran the length of the building, with floor-length windows opening on to it. Colourful climbing plants had been trained at intervals up wooden posts and trellises, almost enclosing the veranda into a garden room. These tumbling plants, though, did not spoil the austere, classical white lines of the house; rather, they softened and humanised it.

The excitement and apprehension—no, *fear*, which she had been feeling at intervals ever since Mr Corrigan's letter had dropped on to her desk was back again. But there was no reason in the world, she told herself stoutly, why she should feel afraid, for there was no way that *anyone* on Halcyon Cay—even people with such sharp grey eyes that they seemed to penetrate effortlessly to her innermost thoughts—should discover who she was . . .

'Please come with me, Miss Lucas.'

The dusky-skinned woman who had answered Cam's rather tentative ring at the doorbell, and who had introduced herself as Miss Poppy, the housekeeper, gave her a comfortable smile as she ushered her through the dim, marble-floored hall. Cam had expected to be taken straight into one of the reception rooms to meet her new employer, but instead she found herself following the neatly dressed woman up a beautiful mahogany staircase, which wound up from the hall in an airy curve.

'I hope you had a pleasant trip, Miss Lucas.'

'Yes, thank you.' Cam smiled back at her with something very like relief. This genuine welcome certainly compared extremely favourably with the half-mocking, half-contemptuous treatment she had received from that man on the boat.

Ahead of her, along the landing, Miss Poppy opened a door, stood back for Cam to enter ahead of her, then crossed the room and threw open one of the pairs of inside shutters which had made it into a pleasantly cool cave, so that it was filled instead with dazzling light.

Cam clasped her hands in unfeigned delight. The room was large, so that the dark, polished furniture was placed far apart, giving it an open, uncluttered feel. There was an old-fashioned high brass bedstead, although the mattress, when she pressed it, was a modern sprung one, and draped over it was a large white mosquito net. An open door to one side showed a turquoise-tiled bathroom, and when the housekeeper opened another door Cam saw the dim outline of a small though delightful-looking sitting-room. She could hardly repress a smile of sheer blissful rapture. She had not just a room, but a whole suite all to herself.

Miss Poppy pulled the shutter half to again. 'I hope you'll be comfortable here, miss.'

'Oh, yes—yes, I'm sure I will,' Cam breathed.

On the dressing-table stood a large wooden bowl filled with fruits, most of which were quite unrecognisable, though they all looked gorgeous, and a vase of white, waxy flowers, their sweet perfume filling the still air. She fingered one of the blossoms.

'Thank you—for putting the flowers and fruit for me, I mean.'

'Oh, Mr Corrigan said for me to do that.'

'Oh.' Somehow, Cam's childhood vision of the ogre-like Matthew Corrigan was undergoing a subtle and disconcerting metamorphosis, for it was not in the least

compatible with *this* Mr Corrigan, who had provided
her with such a pretty suite and ordered flowers and
fruit to be placed in welcome for her.

The housekeeper was surveying, not unkindly, her
hot face and jersey suit. 'Perhaps you would like to
shower, and one of the maids will bring you a cold
drink.'

That sounded marvellous. In the little sitting-room
next door, Cam had caught sight of a small,
comfortable-looking wicker armchair. She could move
it across to the window and loll back at her ease,
catching the cooling breeze from the sea, which she had
glimpsed through the green vegetation that stretched
away down the hill. But no, she reminded herself
sternly, she was not here for a holiday, she was here to
work.

'Doesn't Mr Corrigan want to see me now?'

Miss Poppy shook her head. 'Mr Corrigan will see
you at dinner tonight. He said to tell you that it is served
at six-thirty sharp.'

As soon as the door had closed softly behind her,
Cam kicked off her leather shoes, flexing her toes
gratefully against the cold, mosaic-tiled floor. Mmm.
Old Mr Corrigan must be a bit of a tartar, after all;
there had been a certain imperious inflexion in the
housekeeper's voice, no doubt taken unconsciously
from his command. Oh, well, she would probably see
very little of him once she got down to work; however
much of a hell-raiser he'd been in his day, he must be
very elderly now.

She undressed slowly, shedding her clothes with a
voluptuous delight and feeling the air delicious on her
overheated skin, then went through to the spacious
bathroom. The bath was a huge old-fashioned cast-iron
one, but in one corner, in a tiled alcove, there was a

modern shower, and she stood beneath the cool spray for a long time, sponging herself with the expensive shower gel which smelled delicately of tea-rose and which had also apparently been provided specially for her.

At last, having purged herself of the stickiness and lassitude of her long journey, she wrapped herself in one of the turquoise bath towels and padded back to the bedroom. She had half expected to have to put the jersey suit on again but, as if by some magic sleight of hand, not only had her cases appeared, but her clothes were already hanging up in a wardrobe which smelled faintly of cinnamon and all-spice.

In the room beyond, a shutter had been half opened and a tray put on the low table. There was a glass, a jug of freshly squeezed orange and a bottle of iced mineral water, together with a vacuum jar of ice cubes and silver tongs. Still wrapped in the towel, she mixed herself a long drink and sipped it slowly.

This had obviously been a lady's boudoir; the furniture was so dainty that any mere man would have been frightened away by its prettiness. Perhaps—a strange, choked feeling tightened on her throat—perhaps it had been her grandmother's room—she who had died so young, when Cam's own mother was hardly more than a baby. Maybe if she had lived, who knew—her grandfather might not have set about ruining himself with such reckless abandon. Cam had always, with the pitiless black and white judgement of youth, blamed him, but now, looking round this pretty room . . . She felt her eyes prick suddenly with hot tears, then determinedly drained her glass.

Outside, the swift tropical dusk was already settling over the garden and she glanced at her watch. Oh, no—it was almost six-thirty. What a start! She leapt up and, hurling the towel aside, shot back into the bedroom, then stood in front of the open wardrobe, desperately trying to decide what to wear. She had never taken much interest in fashion, and had prepared for this trip with only the vaguest ideas of what she would need. And now—she bit her lip uncertainly—the house was so much grander, so much more luxurious than anything she had imagined, and old Mr Corrigan, she was certain, would dress up for dinner, in spite of the heat.

But all the clothes she had brought seemed now to be vaguely unsatisfactory, their cool beiges, greys and blues—the colours she favoured at home—dull in comparison with the jubilant riot of colour that now surrounded her. Oh, for heaven's sake! She smiled scornfully at her anxious reflection. Just a few hours in the tropics, and you're well on the way to being seduced by them. And in any case, Mr Corrigan's hardly likely even to be aware of what you're wearing.

She pulled out a pearl-grey and white striped shirt-dress in stiff cotton, dragged it over her head and did up the buttons. Then she hastily ran a comb through her dark gold hair, fixed it into its pleat, gave her ears a quick blast of eau-de-Cologne and tore along the passage and down the staircase, this time all but unaware of its graceful lines as the nervous trepidation churned in her stomach.

Miss Poppy was waiting for her in the hall. As though sensing something of Cam's feelings, she shot her the very faintest smile of reassurance, then ushered her into the dining-room. The room was large and beautifully panelled in a light, honey-coloured wood, which gleamed under the combined wall lights and candles which illuminated the table. But, after a rapid glance, Cam had no eyes for its beauty.

At the far end, french doors stood open to the veranda and, framed in the doorway, glass in hand, stood a man. Cam could have groaned aloud, and her breathing, still flurried from her headlong race downstairs, became even more erratic. So *he* was going to be eating with them, was he? But he mustn't, she wailed inwardly. Those coolly sardonic eyes fixed on her all through dinner—as she was sure they would be—they would undermine totally what little poise she had in these alien surroundings.

But no. She almost gasped aloud with relief. He would not, after all, be joining them. She saw now that only two places had been set, and as he advanced into the room she registered that although he had changed from the faded vest and denims it was only into a casual outfit. The effect, though, she thought reluctantly, was quite something, as fleetingly, from beneath her lashes, she surveyed the length of leg, the grey cords moulded tightly across the flat abdomen and lean thighs, the white cotton shirt setting off the breadth of shoulder and slim waist. She swallowed and hastily removed her gaze, just as he glanced down at his watch with what she knew was a deliberate gesture.

'I thought you were anxious not to blot your copybook by being late.'

'I—I'm sorry.' The apology was out automatically, and too late she snapped her mouth shut on the words, her cheeks burning with angry embarrassment. How dared he reprimand her—and in front of one of the other servants?

He gestured carelessly with his half-empty glass. 'D'you want a drink?'

'No, thank you,' she said formally.

He shrugged, drained his glass, and said past her shoulder, 'You can serve now, Miss Poppy.'

'Very good, sir.'

Cam gave a violent start. *Sir*? Her bewildered eyes flew to his thin, hawk-like face, and she was certain she glimpsed in his eyes a cold malicious gleam. As the housekeeper went out, he drew back a chair for her, with a kind of mocking gallantry that set her teeth on edge.

She waited until he had sat down, then, although pride dictated that she maintain an icy silence, she blurted out, 'W-who are you?'

'Matt Corrigan.'

Across the table, his grey eyes held a challenge that she could not meet. With unsteady hands, she shook out her crisp water-lily napkin and arranged it with extreme care across her knees.

'But I don't understand,' she said slowly at last. 'I thought——' she hesitated, remembering that she must choose her words with great care '—I understood that Mr Matthew Corrigan is an old man.'

'So he was, but he died three months ago at eighty-five. I'm his nephew—and his heir,' he added coolly. 'So, I'm sorry to disappoint you if you'd conjured up a cosy image of some kindly, white-haired old gentleman who would eat out of your hand—though, as far as I can remember of Uncle Matt,' his voice was dry, 'it was the ladies who always seemed to do the eating-out-of-the-hand bit—but I'm afraid that I am, to use that quaint, old-fashioned expression, the master here.'

At first she could only stare at him, her eyes darkening with shock, but finally she said, in a shaky voice, 'The letter—it was from you, then?' In her mind, she saw again that bold, powerful signature. When he merely nodded, she went on, 'I hope you've enjoyed your joke at my expense.'

He shot her a crooked smile. 'Well, as to that, I

hadn't intended deceiving you. But you were such a spiky, superior little madam. Having taken one look at my denims and espadrilles, you cast me in the role of hanger-on, so, not wishing to disappoint you, I went along with your casting. I dare say it was typecasting, anyway,' he grimaced. 'I find I don't fit too well into fancy dress.'

The door opened and a maid, neat in a white cotton print dress, came in carrying bowls of soup while Cam, glad of the chance to remain silent, sat studying the line of hibiscus blossoms which had been arranged down the centre of the table, the soft pink of their delicate trumpets casting a glow on to the dark wood. Of course, if she was honest, she reflected painfully, there had been more than an element of truth in his words. She *had* reacted badly to him, but that had not been through any snobbishness but because with this man, so much more intimidating than any she had ever encountered before, she had responded with the sharp antagonism which was the only weapon available to her against him.

In silence, she picked up her spoon and made a start on her soup, tentatively at first, then enthusiastically as she tasted the delicious creamy lobster bisque. Glancing up, she saw that he was watching her, and she ran her tongue around her lips nervously. She really ought to make an effort to hold some kind of conversation with him, although for his part he was obviously perfectly happy for the oppressive silence to stretch from one end of the meal to the other.

She was still fumbling in her mind for something to say, though, when the maid returned with a dish of chicken in a light, spicy sauce, and rice. She also set down a bottle of white wine, its coldness smoking in the warmth of the room, and he held it out to Cam, his dark brows raised questioningly. She shook her head.

As he poured himself a glass, he said abruptly, 'I hope you'll be up to it.'

'What?' Her jaw dropped slightly and she stared at him in astonishment.

He went on, a shade impatiently, 'I'm paying highly for your services, you know, and I ask myself whether you'll be capable of tackling the job.'

He frowned at her, as though weighing her up, and Cam, her nerves already stretched taut, felt her body stiffen.

'Have you any reason to suppose that I wouldn't be?' she asked, keeping her voice level with a considerable effort.

'No—at least, not yet,' he replied coolly. 'It's simply that I was expecting someone older, more experienced. The tapestries are very valuable, and I don't want any ham-fisted novice ruining them.' He looked her up and down, his eyes gleaming in the soft candlelight. 'You appear very youthful, Miss Lucas, for such a responsibility.'

Very youthful? Of all the nerve. Cam swelled with indignation. 'Oh, I assure you, *Mr* Corrigan,' she said sweetly, 'if, when I see your tapestries——' there was a snap in the final words and she hastily reined herself in '—I doubt my own capabilities to deal with them, I shall inform you at once. But I think my qualifications——'

'Which are?'

She flushed at his tone, angry as much with herself as with him at feeling the need to justify herself to this man, but none the less said, 'A first-class honours degree in embroidery and textiles, a year's postgraduate research where I specialised in seventeenth-century English tapestries and now——'

'And how old are you?'

Really, this was getting to resemble the Spanish

Inquisition. 'I'm twenty-four,' she said briefly.

'But how much have you lived in those twenty-four years?' he mused, almost as though to himself. 'It's my guess that you've led a pretty sheltered existence, kept well away from any of the harsher realities of life.'

She felt the hot anger rising in her again. This was the man who, however unwittingly, was in her place, lording it over her, thanks to the unscrupulous machinations of his uncle. 'I'm afraid you're wrong there,' she burst out impetuously. 'As it happens, I've known quite a few of the harsher realities of life, thanks to——'

She broke off abruptly, terrified of what she might say, and put down her knife and fork, suddenly not hungry any more and determined to sit out the rest of the meal without eating and in silence. But then, as the maid appeared once more, her resolution evaporated. Her sweet was half of a large pineapple, peeled, cored and sliced, then stood on end in its original shape. The flesh had been soaked in some potent liqueur and the centre cavity filled with a tangy lemon water ice. For a moment, the sweet scent reminded her of the last time she had eaten pineapple—tinned chunks, and yes, it had been the evening after that fateful letter had arrived on her desk in that work-room a million miles away. She smiled wryly to herself. Somehow, there could be no better contrast of the then and the now than a dish of syrupy chunks in a down-at-heel London suburb—and this.

She set to work with concentrated enjoyment, and had almost finished when she caught his eye across the table again.

'Good?' he enquired, and she nodded with undisguised pleasure.

'Marvellous. Food for the gods.'

He gave a faint smile. 'Well, perhaps not quite ambrosia, but still, I hoped you'd like it. It's one of the cook's specialities, so I asked her to make it this morning.' He pushed back his chair. 'We'll have coffee on the veranda, I think.'

Outside, the fierce heat of the day had been replaced by a pleasant coolness. Cam lowered herself into a cushioned basket chair and looked around her. Small candle-lamps with glass domes sent a soft, flickering light the length of the wooden veranda; the white blossoms of the creepers which climbed all over the open roof showed as tiny stars, showering their sweet, exotic perfume down on her. A thousand unseen insects crickled softly, and fireflies shimmered green and gold in the darkness of the garden, while beyond, far out in the blackness which glimmered with tiny points of silver, dancing light, were pinpricks which she supposed must be the lamps of fishing-boats.

A vague feeling of disorientation was creeping insidiously through her tired brain. In the white brilliance of day, everything had had a stark reality, but now, in this soft, scented darkness, the world was so—different from everything she knew, so *disturbing*, that for a moment a blind, terrifying panic gripped her so that she felt her leg muscles tense of their own volition, as though to force her to leap up and flee away . . .

The maid padded down towards them, her floppy sandals almost soundless on the polished floor. She set a tray beside them, then withdrew as Matt poured a coffee and handed Cam the fragile old pink and white flowered cup and saucer. She murmured her thanks but, still too shaken by that unnerving sensation that had flooded through her, she could not meet his eyes. He poured two full glasses of Tia Maria liqueur and put one beside her.

Feeling the need of a little support, she took a generous
sip and the mellow, potent fire ran through her. Still
without speaking, he leaned back in his chair, watching
her across the bridge of his long, arched fingers, and she
knew suddenly that he had sensed her panic of a few
minutes before.

'Drink it—it'll do you good. You're very pale.' His
eyes were studying her critically. 'You look very delicate
to me.'

'Oh, for heaven's sake——' she began, then bit her
lip, silencing her irritated retort. 'I'm fine. Just a bit
tired from the flight, and besides, after an English
winter . . .'

'Hmm.'

He sounded doubtful and, stung, she went on, 'Don't
worry. I'm sure I'll be able to cope with your precious
tapestries, Mr Corrigan——'

He held up a hand. 'Please, not Mr Corrigan.
Everyone calls me Matt—so even Miss Camilla Lucas, a
snappish, twenty-four-year-old spinster, complete with
thimble and thread, must do so. But in any case, I
wasn't doubting your credentials any longer.' But was
there not still a touch of mockery lurking beneath the
surface of his apparently reassuring tone? 'No, rather,
it's your ability to stand up to the humidity and the heat
without collapsing in a heap at my feet.'

'There's absolutely no need to concern yourself about
me,' she retorted. 'I'm much tougher than I look, I
assure you, and I'm not in the habit of collapsing at
anyone's feet.' And, she added silently, what's more. I
don't intend to make a start with yours!

With an attempt at insouciance, she drained her
liqueur and leaned back in her chair, but then, as
something large and formless blundered past her head,
she gave a shriek and leapt to her feet. On the wall,

just behind her, a huge—no, *gigantic* black moth, fully nine inches across, had come to rest, its wings still gently vibrating. Cam stared at it, shuddering with horror. Suppose it had flown right into her, tangling itself in the fine silken threads of her hair? Ugh!

Matt uncoiled himself from his chair and she watched in open-mouthed, horrified fascination as his large hands closed over the quivering creature with a gentleness which she would hardly have believed possible. The frantically beating black wings were visible in the cracks between his fingers, and as he turned towards her she took a step backwards.

'It's all right,' he said calmly. 'It's perfectly harmless—just an extra large specimen of a bat moth. No,' as she took another step away from him, 'you mustn't be frightened of it—it's quite harmless. Look.'

He half opened his hands and, fascinated in spite of herself, she stared down at the moth, now quiescent in his hands, seeing for the first time the loveliness of its sooty velvet body, the intricate web of gold and chocolate markings on the huge wings. It raised its fragile antennae, as though in supplication, and he walked to the edge of the veranda, opened his hands and gently flapped the creature away.

All at once, Cam became aware that fatigue was washing over her in a grey tide. She picked up her bag, then hesitated. She wanted nothing more than to climb under the mosquito net and collapse into that pretty brass-framed bed, but maybe she should postpone those delights for a while. Mr Corrigan—Matt had made it abundantly clear that he considered her, through age, inexperience, paleness and no doubt a dozen other things which, if pushed, he could have summoned up, quite unfitted for her task. She would just have to show him his mistake, that was all.

'Off to bed?' he queried.

'No. I'd like to see the tapestries—that's if it's quite convenient for you.'

Matt shrugged. 'OK. If that's what you want, come on, then.'

CHAPTER THREE

IN THE dining-room Matt leaned across the table and picked up one of the branching candlesticks, its candles still alight. As Cam followed him across the entrance hall and down a long, dimly lit passage, a fluttery anticipation filled her, but all at once this was replaced by a feeling almost akin to dread, and for a moment she hung back from him. The candles, held high in his hand, illuminated only one segment of lean, tanned cheek and the top of his head, glinting in the brown hair, and threw his body into dark relief. His limp seemed all at once more pronounced, and his shadow, black and hard-edged against the wall, appeared to be walking alongside him with a menacing life of its own.

For heaven's sake! Cam smiled ruefully to herself. A trick of the light, a few flickering candles, and your imagination is up to all sorts of nonsense. As for menace—well, temporarily, he's your employer, in a formal financial arrangement, and as such he isn't going to menace anybody.

He opened a door and walked into a room, taking the golden halo of candle-glow with him. She followed and stood just inside the doorway, waiting for the room to grow up in front of her as her dilated eyes became accustomed to the darkness. Among the white-shrouded shapes of chairs and sofas there was a table, and he set the candlestick down on to it.

'Sorry about the lack of mod cons,' he remarked, 'but my uncle would never have electricity fitted in this room. He always said that it should only be seen by candlelight.'

There were white shutters all down one wall, tightly closed so that not a gleam of moonlight came through them, but gradually the room was emerging from the shadows for her, and along one wall she could begin to make out, though in outline only, the reasons for her being here. The four tapestries were large, much larger than she had visualised, with a band of solid grey surrounding each, as though it was a huge picture in a frame. But what the contents of the pictures were, her eyes were still unable to make out.

Matt was speaking. 'He used to come in here sometimes, alone, light the candles,' he gestured to two large chandeliers clinking softly above their heads in the gentle draught from the candlestick below, 'and just sit here. When I stayed in the house as a boy, I remember him disappearing in here for hours at a time.'

Cam stared at him tensely, her eyes black in the dim light. She did not want to think of old Matthew Corrigan sitting here, lost in the beauty of the tapestries. That did not square at all with her childhood picture of the man, and for some reason which she did not quite understand she was finding it even more necessary, now that she was actually here, at Tamarind, to keep that angry childhood image intact.'

But then she relaxed. Of course. He wouldn't have been in here wondering at the beauty of the embroidered scenes. No—he would have been laughing to himself, rubbing his hands in renewed delight over his stolen prize . . . And here, facing her, was his heir. Did he now come in here alone, to gloat over these lovely works of art whose colours were just beginning to glow softly in front of her? Of course he did, she thought scornfully. That lean, arrogant face, the mockery lurking in those grey eyes—he looked every bit as unprincipled as the old man must have been. No thought that he had no moral right to the tapestries—or to the house—was ever going to disturb this man's peaceful slumbers.

Slowly, she walked towards the nearest tapestry, fumbling in her bag for the glasses she had taken to wearing for close work. 'He—your uncle did the right thing in keeping out artificial light,' she said, imbuing her voice with an edge of crispness to hide her turbulent feelings. 'I hope the shutters were kept closed most of the time. Strong light could have affected the colours very badly.'

Behind her, Matt gave a derisory snort and she turned to look at him in surprise.

'You could be right,' he said drily, 'but I don't think that was the main reason for keeping this room shuttered and barred. I remember,' his lips twitched slightly in a reminiscent smile, 'one summer—I must have been eleven or twelve—I got very curious about just what this forbidden room contained. So I tried to prise open one of the louvres—that one at the end—from the outside, but the old gardener, who'd no doubt had his orders, caught me and threatened me with a spot of his *obeah*—black magic—if I tried again. So,' he shrugged, 'having an extremely healthy respect for those wicked-looking black cockerels he kept in a pen by his shack, I never tried again.'

But Cam was hardly aware of his words. The azures, pinks and greens of the intricately garlanded flowers and fruits which edged the central picture were now clearly visible and were holding her spellbound. She raised her hand and very gently stroked one finger across a corner swag of fat blush cabbage roses. The artist—for surely it *was* an artist and no mere workaday artisan who had created these masterpieces—had caught the roses at their full, ripe perfection, just one petal slowly falling.

And what was it that these superb borders enclosed? Her eyes had grown accustomed now to the flickering light and she let them travel along the tapestries, but then, as she took in their central theme, her eyes widened in shocked disbelief. Les Amours des Dieux—the Loves of the Gods . . . But it was impossible, quite impossible. She shook her head in bewilderment. All the seventeenth-century tapestry panels in existence dealing with this subject were well-known. Housed in museums, art galleries, country houses, they were all documented, all featured in the definitive works on the great English and European tapestry factories . . . She herself, when she had been a postgraduate student, had helped to repair one single tapestry which had been sent for auction to one of the big London salerooms and which eventually went to a Japanese connoisseur. How on earth could these have remained unknown, unsuspected?

And yet—she looked again at the tapestry before her—these were somehow altogether different from those she was familiar with. In the one that she'd worked on, the god—who was it? Zeus—had been permitted only the faintest smile of triumph as his hands closed on his human prey, while the woman, her pale body flattened and unenticing, bore an expression of alarmed coyness which could not have offended the most prurient taste. She remembered how her tutor had remarked caustically that she was about as much of a turn-on as a bowl of cold porridge.

But these images—they almost leaped at her from the wall, their vitality taking her roughly by the throat as she forced her eyes to travel across them once more . . . Cupid and Psyche, Leda and the Swan, Danaë and

Jove, and—the one just above her head—Europa and
the Bull . . .

Here, there was no pale, soft insipidity which could
safely be hung in any drawing-room . . . Living models
must have been used, not the sketches which the
copyists often employed in their cramped studios. There
was a vibrant intensity in the faces and bodies which
could only have been taken from real life. Europa's
soft, pearly, delicately rounded flesh; Zeus, at the very
moment of transition into the bull, straddling her in all
his potent maleness, his eyes burning with an irresistible
intensity to possess this young girl . . . And yet, for
Cam, it was the girl herself who was even more
shocking. Here, as she lay, her long fair hair outspread
in the daisy-starred grass, there was no terrified
innocence, no chaste, despairing submission to the
inexorable will of the god, but rather a trembling
eagerness which matched his own desire . . .

And the same girl must have been used for the next
frame, where, as Danaë, her pale limbs interlocked with
those of the god, she stared out with blind, unseeing
eyes, her face transfigured in rapturous ecstasy as the
golden shower enfolded her . . . They were, Cam
thought, at one and the same time, some of the most
beautiful works of art she had ever seen—and, in their
naked eroticism, the most deeply disturbing. They were
almost—almost pornographic, saved only by their
beauty and the genius of their creator.

Temporarily, the man behind her had been forgotten,
but now she turned, to find him leaning against the
table, his arms folded. There was a sardonic glint in his
eyes which she did not at all like and she realised that he
had been watching her, awaiting her reaction. Anger
rose in her at the thought that once again he was using
her as a source for his own secret amusement, and to

hide the flush that rose to her cheeks she turned back to the tapestries.

The colours were still wonderful, after more than three hundred years, and yet—she bent to sniff the fabric, and an unpleasant, musty odour came to her. And it wasn't only the effects of the humidity. Here was a small hole—and another, and yes, in the centre of that group of wild strawberries, a large cluster of fraying threads, which had obviously been chewed right through. And then, right before her eyes, a shiny, brown cockroach scuttled out from beneath the fabric. She swung round to face him, her lips tightening.

'How on earth have they been allowed to get into this state? This section——' she slapped her hand against the cloth '—it's absolutely riddled with holes. Your precious uncle, he was nothing better than a philistine—locking them away in here, to gloat over his ill-gotten gains!'

'Oh, and who told you that they were ill-gotten gains?'

His cold, even voice stopped her dead, with a lurch of her stomach, and despite the pallid light she could see the flare of anger in his eyes. Be careful, a tiny voice urged her, or you'll betray yourself—and now, for some reason, it seemed to Cam even more imperative that her identity and connection with Tamarind should be kept a secret. To give herself a moment to recover, she removed her glasses and carefully replaced them in her bag.

'Oh, before I left England,' she said at last, in a careless tone, 'someone told me some story of how he won the house on a hand of cards, having made the previous owner too drunk to know what he was doing.'

The last words were out before she could restrain her tongue, the years of her mother's bitterness adding a caustic edge to them which made him stare at her, his eyes narrowing slightly. All he said though was, 'You seem, Miss Lucas, to have heard a remarkably one-sided version of that event.'

'Oh, have I?'

She willed herself to keep her voice expressionless, but some frisson in her tone must have got through to him, for his voice was even more chill, making her give an involuntary shiver, as he went on, 'Yes, you have. Uncle Matt was a mere nobody, unlike the Forresters, the decadent family who owned Tamarind——' Cam stiffened with outrage and clenched her nails into her hands in the effort not to respond to his contemptuously dismissive tone '—but he was a man of honour. He owned only one thing of value—a pre-Colombian gold and jade statuette that my father had given him before he died—and Forrester wanted it desperately. He suggested the bet—Tamarind and Halcyon Cay against the statuette—and when my uncle held back, he accused him of cowardice.

'He thought he was quite safe, of course—he was the best-known card-sharper in the islands——' fortunately Matt seemed not to notice Cam's smouldering look '—but he lost. Next morning, when they'd both sobered up—yes, you're half right on one point at least—they'd both had rather too much drink that night—Uncle Matt offered to call off the bet, but old Forrester was as proud and stubborn as Lucifer—my uncle's words—and threw the offer back in his face. But it still troubled Uncle Matt's conscience and he sought out the family—there was a child, a girl, I think—in England and tried to give them some compensation, but Forrester would have none of it. Told him to get the hell back to Halcyon Cay and not come near him again.'

Cam felt as though she was standing on perilously

shifting sands. Her whole mind had been thrown into turmoil by his words which, in a few seconds, had undermined every idea that she had grown up with. Matt Corrigan seemed genuinely to believe what he was saying, and yet . . . She shook her head slightly, as though to clear away the fumes of uncertainty that were threatening to seep through the façade of her own beliefs. Yes, how stupid of her. Of course, the old man was bound to have told some such story, in self-justification for his seizure of the estate. And this man—the second generation of Corrigans at Tamarind—well, he would have been only too ready to swallow such a tale, for he too needed justification for his possession, didn't he?

But Matt was still speaking. 'Besides, if it comes to ill-gotten gains,' his steely tone roused her and she raised her eyes slowly to meet his, 'how do you think the original Forrester, back in the seventeenth century, got his thieving hands on them? He stole them, of course.' Somehow, Cam forced down the instinctive protest that sprang to her lips. 'Stole them from a helpless Royalist family that he and his troopers had been billeted on during the Civil War. And then, when the monarchy was restored, this charming character skipped off out here to the estate that Cromwell had given him, leaving his wife and children to follow as best they could, but not forgetting to bring the tapestries with him.'

He gestured towards the wall. 'Funny sort of puritan, don't you think? Hung these in pride of place, and within a few years had had a dozen mistresses and goodness knows how many children. Still,' he shot her a mirthless smile, 'he's not the first person to have been—seduced by the West Indies, and I dare say he won't be the last. What's your opinion, Miss Lucas?'

Cam chose to ignore the question, and the undisguised

provocation behind it. 'All this is beside the point. It was three hundred years ago——'

'Three hundred or thirty, what's the difference?'

'And what matters is that these tapestries,' she carefully did not look at them as she spoke, 'should definitely have been placed in a museum years ago.'

He gave a scornful laugh. 'You mean, they should be locked safely away in a glass case, sterilised and hygienic, where they can't arouse any dangerous thoughts, corrupt any innocents. You look—innocent, Miss Lucas.' His voice had dropped alarmingly to become a deliberate, almost physical caress. 'Do these beautiful pictures threaten to corrupt you?'

Of course they didn't. How could they? She, with her training and experience, was perfectly capable of admiring them solely as superb works of art, wasn't she? And yet, she felt instinctively that there was *something* in this room which was disturbing, almost frightening her, something that was threatening her well-being, her neat, ordered existence . . .

His eyes were holding hers as though in an unspoken challenge. She tore hers free and found them being drawn instead, hypnotically, to the candle flames which, like those darting fireflies earlier, were flickering and dancing up and down in front of her until she was beginning to feel quite dizzy. She put her hand to her head. She really had to—sit—down—for . . .

She was lying in bed, but not in her own familiar bed, with the patchwork quilt, at home. She gathered herself to try to sit up, but then sank back on the pillow with a stifled groan as another wave of dizziness engulfed her. Then a pair of strong hands were hoisting her up, cradling her securely, and someone was putting a glass of icy cold water to her lips. She drank greedily, like a thirsty child, and across the rim she saw—what was she called?—Miss Poppy, standing by the bed.

But if she was over there, who was——? Her teeth clattered against the glass and she pushed it away, then twisted her head up slightly from its resting place against a hard chest, to meet Matt Corrigan's grey eyes.

He held the glass towards her. 'More?'

'N-no, thank you.'

A blush was rising in her cheeks and she turned her head away, but then the blush deepened to scarlet as she realised for the first time that the dress she had worn for dinner was now carefully folded across a chair, while she herself was wearing one of the new cotton nighties she had brought with her. Her eyes flew back to his and she asked huskily, 'Did—who carried me upstairs?'

One corner of his mouth twitched. 'Well, I did tell you that I'm not totally incapacitated.'

Cam was fidgeting with the pink ribbon at her throat. 'And—and who——?'

'Who undressed you? Oh, don't let your maidenly modesty be alarmed. Miss Poppy was here all the time, weren't you?' From out of the corner of her eye, she saw the housekeeper nod. 'So all the proprieties were strictly observed, I assure you, Miss Camilla Lucas.'

Pulling herself clear of him, she laid her head down on the pillow. She closed her eyes momentarily, almost certain that she could feel a prickling electricity where his fingers must have brushed across her unconscious body. He put the side of his hand under her chin and tilted it towards him, the iron strength that she sensed in that hand temporarily masked in gentleness. But she could not resist him, even though she was suddenly all too aware of his warm skin against hers.

'How do you feel now?'

That treacherous blush was rising again. To cover her

embarrassment, and to salvage some pathetic dregs of dignity, she stammered, 'I—I'm sorry—to have been so stupid, I mean. I've never fainted before.'

But he ignored her, only repeating, 'How do you feel?'

'I—I'm fine,' she whispered, but then, as the room began to tilt around her, added, 'I feel very—strange.'

She felt him release his hold on her, then his leg, which she had been pinned against, moved as he straightened up. A hand, which must surely have been Miss Poppy's, very gently brushed against her forehead in a gesture at once so full of comfort and reassurance that she almost turned her head into the pillow and wept. In fact, tears were pricking her eyes, tears of weakness and of vexation with herself. What must he think of her—and after all her fine words about not collapsing at his feet? She must have done just that! And he must certainly now be having the greatest doubts as to whether she'd be able to carry out the work she'd been brought here to do . . .

Voices were in the room with her, floating around her '. . . jet lag . . . an exhausting day . . . the heat . . . a touch of the tropics . . .' a soft laugh '. . . not the first time that a young, unsuspecting girl's been knocked for six by it all . . .'

There were footsteps, which seemed to recede, then come nearer. Her head was being lifted, then somone pushed a pill between her lips. She opened her eyes and squinted up at—Matt, but when she tried to smile at him her features had become stiff and clumsy. All at once, she was being enfolded in a white, hazy cloud, which cocooned her and seemed to be threatening to smother her. For an instant, panic welled up inside her and she fought to sit up, but then she sank back on the pillow as the light was switched off and she heard the door softly close.

She lay still, drifting into a languorous limbo of half-sleep. But then, as she slipped nearer into oblivion, strange visions began flickering behind her eyes, indistinct at first, but all at once with a frightening clarity. The tapestried figures were not safely confined within their embroidered borders any more. They were here, in this room with her, warm, living, flesh and blood, the girl writhing in her voluptuous abandonment, the bull triumphing above her.

Cam's breath quickened in her throat and perspiration broke out on her body as she struggled desperately to break free from the nightmare vision. But, even as she struggled, a terrifying change came over the scene. The young girl's features melted and faded, like some Dali-like fantasy, to be replaced by her own, and at that same moment the bull-god turned to look directly at her. And his face, smiling and darkly menacing, was that of Matt Corrigan.

CHAPTER FOUR

A LIGHT but insistent tapping aroused Cam. She rolled over, stretching luxuriously, as through the white haze of the mosquito net she saw the bedroom door open and Miss Poppy appeared. The housekeeper set down a tray of tea on the bedside table, half opened a shutter, then pulled back the net and peered down at her anxiously.

'How are you this morning, Miss Lucas?'

'Oh, I'm fine, thank you.' And she realised that, miraculously, she was. All the tensions and fatigues, and the final suffocating dizziness which had overwhelmed her in that stifling, candelit room the previous night—it had all vanished. Just for a moment, the shadow of her terrifying nightmare brushed across her consciousness again, like the touch of that moth's soft wings, and she shivered, but then that too had gone, and she was filled with a totally unaccustomed buoyant energy.

Miss Poppy looked relieved. 'That's good, miss. We were so worried about you. Mr Corrigan, he tell me we must send for the doctor at Port Charlotte if you not better. He say, she such a delicate little thing, how will she ever manage the work?'

Cam, who had been about to indulge in another lazy head-to-toe stretch, sat up immediately and reached for the cup of tea.

'Well, you can tell him I'm quite recovered, Miss Poppy,' she said firmly.

'And would you like breakfast here or out on the

veranda downstairs?'

Cam hesitated. She would have much preferred the cool morning air of the veranda, but on the other hand . . .

'Mr Corrigan say he see you later, but he has gone out already this morning.'

Cam smiled warmly up at her. 'I think I'll eat outside, thank you, Miss Poppy.'

A huge old tree at the end of the veranda dripped tiny red petals like drops of nectar, showering the breakfast tray and the polished floor. One, like a scrap of scarlet silk, drifted on to her bare arm and she picked it up and blew it gently away.

She followed the orange juice and toast with a fruit from the bowl, which looked like a cross between a ripe orange and a large tangerine but was more delicious than either, then poured herself a second cup of the strong, fragrant coffee and leaned back in the comfortable chair. The coconut palms rustled gently in the warm breeze, the soft shush of the waves on to the beach below wafted up to her. Paradise. She could happily sit here, letting the whole morning slide unnoticed away from her . . .

Cam sat bolt upright, drained her cup, and got to her feet. Really, she simply had to stop forgetting constantly that she was here, not as some pampered tourist, but to work. It just wasn't right for her to lounge around like this any longer—besides which, the man who was employing her on such excellent financial terms would without doubt find some highly caustic remark with which to indulge himself if he were to find her here, sprawled at her ease.

In the tapestry salon, her vinyl bag had been placed ready for her. Although beads of perspiration were

already forming on her brow, she determinedly took out
her grey drill overall and pulled it on over the businesslike navy cotton dress which she had brought as her
work outfit. She bundled her hair into an old chiffon
scarf, then grimaced abruptly as she caught a glimpse of
the drab picture she made in the large gilt mirror that
hung on one wall.

The step-ladder she had asked for was propped by the
door. She fished out her notebook and pencil from her
bag, put on her glasses, then, manoeuvring the steps
alongside the nearest tapestry, set to work. All this time,
she had deliberately not looked at the tapestries in their
disturbing entirety, and gradually she forgot about their
content as she became totally absorbed in her detailed,
thread by thread examination of each minute section.

The iced drink that a maid brought in stayed
untasted, until at last she straightened up reluctantly, to
ease her stiff back. Now that she had broken off her
survey, she realised that her dress was sticking to her,
and she was rapidly becoming too uncomfortable to
work. She just couldn't stay in this completely
unsuitable outfit. She softly opened the door and risked
a quick look, but the corridor was quite deserted, so she
rapidly tore open the fastening of her overall, tossed it
on to the table, then unbuttoned her dress and stepped
out of it. Clad only in her pretty white cotton bra and
pants, she was just reaching for the overall again when
behind her she heard the faintest of sounds.

She spun round, then her violet eyes dilated hugely
with shock as she saw, lounging against a small door let
into the wall panelling and which she had not even
noticed before, Matt Corrigan. Arms folded, he was
surveying her with undisguised interest. For a frozen
instant she stared at him, then simultaneously one arm
flew protectively across her breasts, while with the other

hand she snatched up the overall and held it to her.

Casually he straightened up and, as he began to walk unhurriedly towards her, she hastily backed away, fetching up hard against the scalloped edge of the mahogany table. Although he did not speak, there was, momentarily, an intensity about his expression which deeply unnerved her. But when he came up to her, he merely said, 'Feeling the heat, Miss Lucas?'

'I—I—yes,' she stammered, furious with herself as she felt the hot blush seemingly spreading from her face to the very tips of her toes, and equally furious with him for so obviously relishing every moment of her discomfiture.

'I thought for a moment you'd stepped down off one of the tapestries.' His eyes glinted. 'You know—"Nymph Surprised While Bathing".'

Cam's hands tightened convulsively as his apparently flippant words reawakened for her, with terrifying vividness, the warm throb of sensuality that had stolen over her in that half-sleeping, half-waking dream. But then, even as she struggled to thrust the memory from her, he continued in the same matter-of-fact tone, 'And talking of bathing, you're quite welcome to use the swimming pool in the grounds, you know. In fact, why don't you cool off with a bathe before lunch?'

'Oh, no—no, thank you,' she said quickly. The idea of limpid water lapping her overheated body was most enticing, but if she agreed he might well choose to join her and she quailed at the very thought.

He shrugged offhandedly. 'OK, but feel free to use it this afternoon if you want to.'

'But I'll be getting on with the work after lunch.'

Matt shook his head firmly. 'Nobody works out here in the early afternoon. It's far too hot. You're not on a nine-to-five job now, you know. You'll have to take a break and start again when it's cooler—about four. So, if you feel like a bathe, be my guest.'

But I'm not your guest, thought Cam with a fierce little spurt of resentment. I'm your employee, expected to be humbly grateful for any crumb of favour you choose to throw my way. But then, she reminded herself, to do him justice he was quite unaware of her true situation and, far from patronising her, he had no doubt been attempting, with the attractive suite of rooms, the flowers, to make her feel at home, without the slightest suspicion that, in other circumstances, Tamarind would indeed have been her home. And yet, she thought ruefully, every time she came into close proximity with his disturbing presence, being comfortably at her ease was the very last sensation in the world which she was capable of feeling.

'How are you this morning?'

She came out of her thoughts to an awareness that he was eyeing her keenly. 'Oh, much better, thanks,' she said briefly, not wishing to reawaken thoughts, let alone speak of the previous night.

'Hmm. Well, you certainly look better than you did last night.'

Did his lips ever so faintly twitch with secret amusement? Cam couldn't be quite sure but, forced to remember whose hands had almost certainly so deftly undressed her and put her into her nightdress, she felt the blush rise to her cheeks again, as she responded constrainedly, 'I'm sorry to have made such a fool of myself.'

'That's all right. Jet lag can hit anybody.' Although Cam was quite certain that it would never dare to hit Matt Corrigan. He glanced at his watch. 'I must go. I shan't be joining you for lunch, I'm afraid.' A surge of intense relief swept through her at his words, which she hoped she managed to conceal. 'I've got to go across to St Hilaire on business, but I should be back for dinner.' He gestured towards the tapestries. 'Perhaps you'll be good enough to give me a résumé then of your findings so far.' And abruptly, he had gone.

For several moments, Cam stood quite still. Then, as the slow realisation came that she was still clutching the overall to her, she roused herself, dragged it quickly down over her head and shoulders and, with hands that were not quite steady, fastened it up. Somehow, though, the happy impetus which had made the morning melt away unnoticed had completely disappeared now. Still, she ought to get on. She picked up her notebook and pencil again, and put her hand on the step-ladder, but then, glancing at her watch, she saw that it was after midday. She might just as well pack up now; then, whatever Matt had said, she would start work again, refreshed by the break, as soon as lunch was over.

Upstairs, she showered, put on the dress she had so unwisely discarded in the tapestry room, and went back downstairs. Lunch—consommé, followed by tangy, marinated strips of some delicious fish with salad, then fruit—was served for her out on the veranda, where the faint breeze, blowing in from the sea, had a delightful coolness against her warm skin. One of the maids brought her a tray of coffee, and Cam sipped it, avidly drinking in at the same time the unclouded blue sky and against it the feathery, undulating tops of the coconut palms and the green lacework of the acacias and jacaranda trees.

All this beauty. If only . . . if only . . . Cam sighed softly, then came out of her daydream, abruptly dismissing the picture of the might-have-been from her mind. It's no use, my girl, she told herself sternly, as she went slowly upstairs. Tamarind does not belong to the

Forresters; it belongs to Matt Corrigan. And there, if
ever, is a man who, while certainly no crook, would
hold on to what he considered lawfully his with a grip of
steel.

Her high-ceilinged room, the shutters almost closed,
was a welcoming cavern, the white bedspread an
irresistible invitation to flop down just for a moment
while she . . .

The high-pitched scolding of a bird in a tree outside
roused her, and when she managed to focus on her
watch she saw that she had slept for almost two hours.
She stretched and sat up with a shame-faced smile. All
her good intentions! But even now she was shocked to
realise that she felt a strange, heavy reluctance to go
back to that silent room downstairs and continue her
painstaking, inch by inch scrutiny of the precious
fabric. She must still be ever so slightly jet-lagged. Yes,
that was it. By tomorrow, all her old enthusiasm and
pleasure in her work would have returned.

Now, though—perhaps that bathe which Matt had
suggested would lift her out of her lethargy. When she
pushed open the shutter at the far end of her room and
leaned dangerously out, she could just see one portion
of what must be the pool, round the corner of the
house, behind a white, fretwork stone wall and a screen
of pink oleanders. Its surface was like a turquoise
mirror, unruffled, smooth as silk. No one was there, she
was sure. And then she remembered—Matt had said
that he would not be back until dinner at the earliest.

She found her swimsuit in the drawer, where the maid
had placed it, and slipped into it, then stood biting her
lower lip and regarding herself critically in the long
mirror. Its colour—plain dark green—was fine, and it
was a one-piece. But still—she frowned with dissatis-

faction—all the swimsuits seemed to be cut so high these
days, and this one, although it had been the least hacked
away she could search out, was still so high at the sides that
her legs, already long and slim, looked almost
embarrassingly so. Oh, well, she shrugged slightly, at least
for this first bathe she would have the pool to herself. She
put on the pale blue towelling wrap that covered her
chastely from neck to knees and went downstairs.

None of the staff were around and she eventually
found her own way out of a side door to see ahead of
her the white, airy screen of walling which encircled the
pool. At the far end was a gap, masked by more
oleanders and a huge bed of tall canna lilies, thrusting
upwards their huge, flame-coloured heads of bloom,
like ranks of naked spears. If Cam had not been giving
their exotic beauty all her attention, she would have seen
him earlier.

As it was, she was through the gap and standing on
the pale smooth stone surround of the pool before she
realised that, just two yards from her, sprawled on a
padded lounger, was Matt Corrigan. There was a half-
empty glass beside him and a book, tossed carelessly
down, but he was lying back, seemingly asleep.

Perhaps she had time to escape. Cam, her eyes fixed
on him, took a furtive step backwards; her sandal heel
crunched down on the stone edging of the bed of lilies
and she saw Matt spring into wakefulness. His head
jerked round and just for a second she glimpsed, to her
surprise, not exactly fear, but an alert, wary tension.
Then, as he saw her, a faint, almost wry smile flickered
across his lips, and he relaxed back against the chair.

'Come and join me.'

His tone was lazy enough, but there was a hint of
steely command beneath the surface which she did not
quite dare to resist, and she walked slowly across to

him. A second lounger was near his—too near—but when she put her hand on it to edge it slightly further away, his hand, which had been resting on it as though in invitation, tightened its grip so that she could not budge it.

She stared down at him. 'You said you weren't coming back until later.' Too late, she registered the note of accusation in her voice, sparked by the annoyance she felt at his unexpected presence.

He raised one sardonic eyebrow. 'Oh, I'm sorry. I hadn't realised that I have to consult you before changing my plans. I'll try and remember in future.'

She flushed at the stinging rebuke, at the same time conscious that he was right. She was, after all, his employee, and employees—if they knew what was good for them—did not question the movements of their new employers.

But then he went on more mildly, 'Actually, I got through the business with my lawyer much quicker than I'd expected. For once, Bob Latham was in a hurry so he wasn't as long-winded as usual. His niece, Cathy Devinish, and her husband are arriving on the afternoon flight from England, to show Bob and his wife their new baby. So I took the chance to escape—and besides, it seemed, for some reason, a good idea to get back here.'

'Oh.' Cam smiled uncertainly, confused by the apparent undercurrent, almost of challenge, in his voice. She hesitated a moment, her hands at the belt of the towelling wrap, then with one quick, jerky movement slipped out of it and dropped it on to the ground.

As she straightened her eyes slid fleetingly to his, then momentarily she stilled, an electric shock shivering through all her limbs. His gaze was travelling slowly up her body, taking in, in frank appraisal, her slim legs, the long curve of her thighs, so accentuated by the high cut of her green swimsuit, and upwards to the soft fullness of her breasts.

That same expression which she had seen that morning in the tapestry salon had returned, but with a far greater intensity, and now she knew it for what it was. Although she had never seen such an expression in a man's eyes before, she recognised the sexual desire which had flared nakedly in those grey eyes. Just for a moment, she glimpsed a dark underworld of passion, and a strange exultation swelled inside her with the knowledge that she possessed this totally unsuspected power to arouse such a passion.

But then this feeling was swept aside by a blind terror. Such powers, she knew instinctively were dangerous and could hurtle her, totally inexperienced as she was, to her absolute destruction. She simply wasn't ready to be desired in this way, by this man. Once again, she felt her nightmare of the night before and reality blurring and blending together, and the panic swirled within her . . .

Hardly aware of what she was doing, she took a half-step backwards, her hands raised, palms outstretched as though to ward off a physical assault. But the expression had faded from Matt's eyes and as her breathing steadied she slid quickly down on to the lounger.

In contrast to her inner turmoil, his voice, as he poured her a drink, was quite steady. 'Don't worry. It's only lime—nothing stronger.' He dropped in two ice-cubes and passed it to her. 'How's the work going?'

'Oh, all right.' An ice-cube tinkled against the rim of her glass as she took a determined mouthful of the tart, cool juice. 'I haven't finished checking the tapestries in detail yet, but I think I'll be able to deal with them here. I won't—I mean, *you*,' she corrected herself hastily, 'won't have to send them off the island for treatment. But I'm just afraid that the work may take longer than was envisaged. It obviously can't be hurried.'

Matt shrugged carelessly. 'No problem. Take as long as you like.'

'But my job in England,' Cam protested. 'And besides——' She broke off abruptly. She had been about to say that her mother would be expecting her back, but that sounded altogether too feeble, and instead she went on, 'I'm due back at the museum in three months at the absolute latest. We've got a big restoration project starting in——'

'I'm sure they'll manage without you. If necessary, I'll get in touch and arrange an extension of your secondment. There'll be no difficulty.'

No difficulty? Maybe not, Cam thought. In fact, even knowing this man as little as she did, she was quite certain he would arrange absolutely anything he wanted to his complete satisfaction . . . And yet—no difficulty? There was a twist of that insidious fear again—if she stayed here for the three months, let along longer, who knew what difficulties, even dangers, might confront her?

They both lapsed into silence, but Cam at last felt herself driven to break this silence, nervous and brittle as it was on her side, however relaxed it might be on his.

'Have you lived at Halcyon Cay long?' Her voice was stilted, but at least the question was better than nothing.

'Oh, on and off since I was a child. But I've only been settled here a couple of months.'

She sensed a frisson of angry frustration behind the words, but she went on, 'Since you inherited the property, I suppose?' She was amazed at how casual she sounded.

'Yes, but that's not the only reason,' he replied brusquely, as though to put a swift end to this obviously unwelcome topic. But Cam, under a sudden compulsion to learn all she could of the Corrigan clan who had driven her family from its earthly paradise, pressed on.

'Your uncle—he had no children?'

Matt laughed. 'Well, not exactly—but none to inherit. He never married. My father was his younger—much younger—brother. He married a Mexican girl.' So she had been right. The intensely dark brown hair, the narrow, hard-planed face, the subtle hint of cruelty in his lips—were there even, she wondered, a few drops of Aztec blood lurking somewhere beneath that deeply bronzed skin?

'But they died when I was ten, and Uncle Matt—I was named Mateo in his honour—took over as my guardian and brought me up—after his own inimitable fashion.' A wry note entered his voice. 'I was boarded at private schools in the States, but I spent all my vacations here, where I was allowed absolute freedom to run wild.' And there was still more than a hint of that wildness, Cam thought involuntarily. '—And I'm thirty-four years old, not married, never have been and never likely to be.'

At the sudden, harsh cynicism in his tone, Cam's eyes flew to his face, but his expression was quite impassive.

'So, does that satisfy your girlish curiosity, Miss Camilla Lucas?' She flushed at his caustic tone, but then, disarmingly, he pulled a face. 'That makes you sound like something out of a Jane Austen novel. I can't call you Miss Lucas, or even Camilla, if you're going to be staying under my roof for months. So, *Cam*,' he straightened up, 'are you coming for that bathe?'

She pressed herself down more firmly into the soft upholstery. Suddenly, the limpid blue water, so inviting from her bedroom window, was not nearly so enticing now.

'N-no, not just yet, thank you.'

He stood up, shrugged off his white T-shirt and stepped out of his canvas jeans. As he turned to drop them on to the lounger, his knees were virtually on a level with her eyes. For the first time, Cam saw his legs bare and her eyes widened in horror as she caught sight of his right knee. It was defaced by the ugly pattern of red, still angry-looking ridges of scar tissue which criss-crossed it, puckering the skin horribly into seams which radiated up and down into his thigh and lower leg. Shocked, she stared up at him and his lips twisted.

'Not a pretty sight, is it? Still, I'm lucky, apparently, not to have lost the leg.' Cam shuddered as he went on, with the faintest shadow of a rueful grin, 'I gather it took quite some stitching together. What a pity you weren't around to work on me with your needle and thread.'

A spasm of nausea gripped her stomach at the appalling image his words conjured up. 'But—but was it an accident?'

'I imagine so.' His tone was dry. 'They were no doubt aiming for my heart.'

Then, as Cam gaped at him, stunned into silence, he turned, walked slowly away from her to the deep end of the pool and dived, cutting into the water as cleanly as a swift, brown arrow. He surfaced yards away, tossing back his hair in a shower of droplets, the water gleaming on his polished skin. From beneath her lowered lashes, Cam watched in helpless fascination as he did several lengths of fast crawl, clearly exulting in the sheer animal pleasure as he scythed through the rippling surface. He might still have a slight awkwardness on land, but his knee certainly did not impede him in the slightest in the water. At the end of each length he would corkscrew down to turn like some lithe, sleek otter, then, although she was seemingly forgotten in his obvious physical enjoyment, he would surge back down the pool towards her.

Those powerful brown shoulders and arms, cutting through the turquoise wavelets . . . What must it be like to be held in those arms, to be cradled possessively—no, *hungrily*, by Matt Corrigan? Cam caught her breath in a little, shuddering gasp. What utter madness, what fantastic tropical daydream was she indulging in now? She tried to smile at herself, mocking her own folly, but it was no use. She had to get away—back to work. Yes, that was it. She must find sanctuary in that quiet, shuttered room, where those tapestries hung, waiting for her careful attentions.

Blindly, she fumbled beside her for her bag and robe, then scrambled to her feet and began to walk rapidly down the side of the pool.

'Hey!' Matt's peremptory call held her unwillingly. She turned slowly, not able to look directly at him, but seeing him swim across towards her to tread water just beneath her feet. 'Where the hell are you racing off to?'

'I-I'm going to start work again.'

She heard the husky tremor in her own voice and, angry with herself, went to turn away.

'Put your bag down.'

'What?'

Puzzled, Cam stared down at him, but his face was expressionless, his eyes telling her nothing.

'Put your bag down.' He gestured with his head towards the tiles and, obedient to the command in his voice, she stooped to drop her bag. 'The work will wait. You've really got to learn, Cam, to relax, to let go. You came out for a swim, so come on in.'

'No, I've changed my——'

Too late, she caught the warning glint of devilry that

now leapt into his eyes, and too late, as his hand snaked out of the pool towards her, she tried to jerk back out of reach. Long, predatory fingers had already curved around one slim ankle, closing on it, and now, before she could even cry out, with one quick wrench he toppled her clean into the water beside him.

Caught right off balance, Cam fell headfirst, helpless to save herself, and came up hard against ten feet of water. The towelling robe she was still clutching soaked up the water like a thirsty sponge and, wrapping itself horribly around her legs like the tentacles of some sea monster, dragged her under. Powerless to save herself, she was falling away from the sun-dappled surface into the darker depths, the water filling her eyes, her ears, her lungs, and she was going to drown . . .

From nowhere, hands came out and caught her round the waist, pulling her in close against a hard, muscled body, and enfolding her against it so that, though she struggled frantically against her captivity, she was a securely held prisoner. Then she was dragged swiftly upwards, until hot sunlight was burning against her closed eyelids, and as she broke the surface, coughing and spluttering, she was at last able to snatch in a deep gulp of air.

Matt was still holding her close against him, and when finally she opened her drenched eyes it was to see his face only inches from her own, as he effortlessly trod water to keep them both afloat.

'Th-that was a stupid thing to do!' she gasped furiously.

He shook her slightly. 'Why in heaven's name didn't you tell me you can't swim!'

'I-I can!' In the midst of another choking fit, Cam could just about manage the indignant retort.

He gave a snort of laughter. 'You didn't seem to be

showing much inclination to do so ten feet down.'

Cam shot him a look of pure loathing. 'Well, I can.' No need to tell him that she could manage one width, or a careful length with a big toe hovering near the bottom. 'Anyone caught off balance like that would—would——'

'Would flounder about like an elephant in a mud hole?'

She flung him another smouldering glare and pushed down hard on his arms to release herself, but he merely tightened his hold on her, bringing their faces even closer together.

'Has anyone ever told you what a quite remarkable pair of eyes you have?' As Cam, completely nonplussed, could only stare back into his own intense grey eyes, the irises almost black, ringed with charcoal, she felt her chest muscles tighten strangely, as though she had been plunged back under the water. 'Soft violet eyes, but they darken to pansy purple when you're angry, I see. You should get angry more often, Cam. Though I wonder,' his voice dropped so that it was almost like a caress on her face, 'what entrancing shade they might be, if someone were to arouse other—passions in you.'

Cam's head jerked back as though he had physically struck her, but there was no escape. While one hand slid down her back, moulding her tightly into his body, his lips came down on hers, which were already opening for the angry protest which never came, and closed over them. She wanted to fight, to kick, to break free, but the sweetness of his mouth, the smell of his skin—an unfamiliar, warm male perfume—the strength of his hard body against her softness, all acted like mouthfuls of neat cognac on an empty stomach, running through her like mellow fire, warming her into vital life, until flames seemed to lick through her, scorching her nerve-endings in sensations so totally devastating that she could only let go, closing her eyes and surrendering herself to them utterly.

CHAPTER FIVE

BUT then, from somewhere—from one far distant recess of her mind—cold, lucid sanity came gushing back. Cam forced her mouth from his and dragged her head away.

'Don't! Let me go,' she pleaded, but Matt's grip did not in the slightest slacken.

'I've told you, Cam, don't be so uptight—you've got to learn to relax.'

His voice was a husky whisper in her ear, and she struggled fiercely to escape, dragging both of them down into the water again. This time, he took a firm grasp of her upper arms and pulled her none too gently to the side of the pool, where she clung on to the rail.

'I said relax—not do your best to drown us both.'

He lifted a heavy strand of wet hair which had streaked across her face, and tucked it behind her ear. The casual touch of his fingers brushed an insidious, tingling trail across her cheek and she jerked her head back once more. She had to break free, not only physically, but from the potent spell which—deliberately or unconsciously, she could not guess which—he was rapidly weaving around her.

'L-look Matt——' she began uncertainly, forcing herself to face him squarely. But then, as she caught the gleam of mockery in his eyes, her lips tightened and she went on, her voice tightly controlled. 'Let's get one thing straight right from the beginning, can we? You're paying me—and very well too, as you've already pointed out . . .' She faltered for a moment as he brought down his dark level brows in a frown, then hurried on, '—to do a job, and one job only. I'm here to repair your tapestries, and nothing else. I know you think I'm a prim little prude——' Her voice wobbled as suddenly, enragingly, she felt herself on the brink of tears, but she forced herself to continue. After all, why should she care one iota for what he thought of her? 'And maybe I am, but I've no intention of being your—your latest plaything.' The frown deepened to an angry scowl and, shaken by her own temerity, Cam floundered on, 'I—I hope you understand what . . .'

'Oh, I understand you quite well.' When she flashed him a lightning look from beneath the security of her lashes, she saw that Matt's lips had thinned to a chilling line. 'Thank you for making your—position,' the faint slur on the word brought the hot colour momentarily back to her cheeks, 'so perfectly clear.'

But he didn't understand. He didn't in the least understand. How she had never met a man like him before. How he made her feel—apprehensive, even afraid, in a way she had never felt before. But how could she possibly even begin to try to explain the maelstrom of her feelings to him? He would no doubt merely despise her even more.

'I'm sorry——' she began, but he cut in brutally.

'Oh, never apologise, Cam. Didn't you know—it's a sign of weakness? And now, as you so kindly reminded me. I'm paying very highly for your services, so—when you're quite ready, of course—I suggest that you return to those tapestries which you find so fascinating.'

Smarting under the lash of his bored, dismissive tone, she swung away from him in silence, and swam at a speed she had never in her life achieved before to the steps at the shallow end of the pool. She hauled herself out and, quite unable to trust herself to speak, or even look at him, bent to snatch up her bag. Her towelling wrap lay in a sodden heap at the bottom of the pool, but it would just have to remain there. Out of the corner of her eye, she saw Matt turn and swim towards the far side of the pool with quick, impatient strokes, then she walked rapidly away, her light, hurried footsteps echoing off the tiles.

She closed her bedroom door and leaned against it, grateful for its solid support. Then, aware of the steady drip of water from her sopping swimsuit, she slowly straightened, went through to the bathroom and peeled it off. Not bothering to dry herself, she sat on the edge of the bath, gripping its hard edge with both hands and staring at the wall tiles opposite her. Lethargically, she traced the convoluted whorls of turquoise pattern round and round and round, through to the heart of each, as dark misery welled up inside her.

What a fool she'd made of herself. What must he think of her—and yes, she acknowledged, she *did* care what he thought—acting as she had like a foolish girl or, worse, like the timid spinster he so clearly thought her? Cam gave a stifled groan at the memory of how she had reacted—no, over-reacted, to what to Matt was surely just a piece of harmless fun. If only she were more experienced with men, she could have handled the situation with cool, dignified poise, instead of—— Cam gulped, and to her surprise felt a tear roll down her cheek and plop on to her bare thigh.

And yet, she told herself, as she fiercely flicked it away, she was right. However clumsily she had behaved, she had been right to make him understand, right from the beginning, that she was not prepared to indulge in some trivial, meaningless sexual escapade, merely to help him while away his obviously enforced idleness. *She was right*. Any emotional entanglement with Matt Corrigan was, for someone like her, just too dangerous. He was clearly frustrated by the captivity his injury had imposed on him. The coiled tensions within him almost made the air around him hum, a chained tiger chafing at his prison bars—no matter how idyllic that prison was. But, when the injury had finally healed and he was at liberty once more, where would that leave her, if she had been so utterably foolish as to——?

And yet, she could still feel the taste of his lips as they hungrily explored her mouth, still faintly smell that warm, sensual male aroma of his skin on hers . . .

Cam leapt to her feet. Work. That was her salvation. Not the relaxing, the letting go that Matt had urged on her, but hard, unremitting work. After all, that would be no problem, she thought, as she showered swiftly, coiled her wet hair inside the chiffon scarf and firmly fastened herself into her overall. She loved her work, had never, as long as she could remember, wanted to do anything else, and the tapestries presented the greatest challenge she had ever faced. What a sense of achievement she would have when, her task successfully completed, she caught the plane home to London.

To Cam's intense relief, Matt seemed to have come to much the same conclusion. He did not intrude again into the tapestry salon that evening, although all the time she was there her nerves were set jangling at the slightest sound, and then, over dinner, he was coolly correct.

And so the pattern of her life at Tamarind developed. Every morning, as soon as she had finished a solitary breakfast, she would put on her overall and get down to work. Each afternoon, after a rest, she would bathe in the garden pool—after that first day, seemingly by tacit agreement, Matt was never there. Most evenings, he would join her at dinner, but his small talk was icily formal.

Occasionally, he would ask for a report on the progress of her work, and at her request he organised a group of estate workers to lift down the first tapestry from the wall so that she could begin the restoration work. Standing in the far corner of the room, he watched in silence while she spread the nylon gauze over the first section and pinned it into place before, with the utmost delicacy, she ran her battery-operated vacuum cleaner over it, to remove the surface debris of centuries. At first, her hands trembled slightly under the combined tension of his austere presence and the responsibility of her undertaking but then, gradually, she became engrossed in her task. She did not know how much later it was when she paused and glanced round, but he had gone.

As the days went by, though, she would increasingly catch herself staring unaccountably into space, her needle suspended in mid-air, and she would angrily rouse herself from her reverie to return to her work. Her innate common sense told her that she should be thankful that Matt's attitude was making it so much easier for her to carry out her resolve and yet, time and again, in the salon, in the gardens, by the pool, she found herself listening for his footsteps, straining her ears to catch the distant sound of his voice.

Although she tried desperately to prevent her thoughts from ever straying back to that first afternoon, she could not prevent herself recalling, with no lessening of her initial bewilderment, Matt's dry, unemotional response to her naïve question about his injured knee: 'An accident? I imagine so. They were no doubt aiming for my heart.'

They? Who could he mean? In that so-brief period of

intimacy, however limited, between them, she had found it almost impossible to read this enigmatic man, but she was quite certain that, in this matter at least, he had been deadly serious. But what did he mean by it? What kind of life-style did his words hint at? Professional soldier? Anti-narcotics agent? Some of the Caribbean islands were reputed to be staging-posts for drug smugglers . . . She couldn't hope to guess, but she felt instinctively that, whatever life he led—and was so impatient to return to—there could be no place in it for an unworldly English seamstress . . .

And that made it all the more imperative that she complete her work here as rapidly as possible. The trouble was that the task was proving to be even more demanding than she'd realised, requiring such meticulous care at every stage that she was progressing with frustrating slowness and was increasingly falling behind her original optimistic, self-imposed schedule.

So, one afternoon, after snatching a hasty lunch, she did not take her usual rest or even bathe, but went straight back to the salon. For the past few days now, she had been engaged on the delicate task of washing the second tapestry—a task she much preferred to omit, if possible, but all four of the hangings were so grimed with the dirt of centuries that it had to be done. If she stuck at it all afternoon, she should finish and then be able to move on to the actual repair stage.

Miss Poppy had provided her with a large bowl of distilled water, and Cam carefully dissolved some soap-flakes in it, then with a soft sponge began methodically stroking the back of the fabric. It was very hot, with not a breath of air coming through the half-opened shutters. Soon rivulets of sweat were trickling from her neck and underarms, and her fingers had developed soggy crinkles.

'Having problems?'

She had been straining in a vain effort to reach an area towards the centre, and started, almost knocking over the bowl.

'No, I'm managing perfectly, thank you,' she replied levelly, squeezing the sponge tightly without turning round.

'Hmm. It looks a pretty hazardous operation to me. Are you sure you won't rot the fabric?'

This time, Cam looked up sharply, to see Matt lounging against the table, his hands in his jean pockets.

'Quite sure.' She managed to keep her voice still perfectly even. 'It's quite safe if—*when* you know what you're doing.'

He held up his arms in mock surrender. 'OK, OK, I wasn't getting at you. You really must develop a thicker skin and stop suspecting that every word I say is a hardly veiled insult.'

And whose fault is it if I do? she wanted to say. Instead she merely turned back and stolidly went on with her work. After a few minutes, though, she risked a look under her arm and saw that those long, jean-clad legs had gone. He must have been bored, she thought, and decided to while away a happy afternoon disconcerting her, but at least she'd stood up to him and he'd wisely taken the hint.

The door opened and Matt appeared, sponge in hand. As she gazed in horror from him to the sponge and back he gave her a disarming grin.

'Well, you did look as if you could do with an extra pair of hands, or at least a longer arm.' He must have caught sight of her expression, for he added, 'This looks the sort of job even a complete incompetent like me can do—under your expert tuition, of course.'

Was he getting yet another rise out of her? Cam eyed him narrowly, but there was not even a glint of mockery or provocation in those bland grey eyes, so she merely shrugged.

'You can't kneel on the floor. It's too hard,' she said brusquely, and reaching an old towel out of her workbag she folded it and slid it along the polished floor to the far corner of the tapestry. 'Don't try to cover too big an area at once, stroke the cloth rather than rubbing at it—that brings the dirt to the surface. Oh, and you mustn't soak it or it really will rot.'

He nodded obediently but then, with his foot, tweaked the towel back beside her own kneeling pad. When she looked at him, he said briefly, 'Only one bowl, and my arms aren't quite in the gorilla league.'

They worked in silence, side by side, for some time. Matt seemed to lose himself almost at once in what he was doing, working with apparent total absorption, but Cam's concentration was quite shattered. Every fibre in her body sensed him beside her; she could see him out of the corner of her eye, she could smell the faint citrus of his aftershave. Once, their fingers met among the soapy suds and she withdrew her tingling hand as though the water was scalding hot.

Much later, she shot him a furtive glance from under the safety of her lashes. He was leaning forward, frowning in total concentration, his hair falling forward over his eyes, that slightly over-long black lock which curled endearingly into the nape of his neck . . . Horror-stricken, Cam realised that her fingers were almost twitching under the urge to stroke that half-curl, twine it gently around her finger. Abruptly, she pushed herself back on her heels, put down her sponge and reached for the bowl.

'What are you doing?'

'I—the water's too dirty. I'll get some more.'

But he put his hand on her wrist. 'No, you've done enough for today.'

'No, I want to finish this corner,' she protested. 'It won't take very long.'

But when she went to lift the bowl his hand tightened its grip. 'I said *no*. You're not doing any more.'

He uncoiled himself rather stiffly, then before she could duck away from him he had lifted her to her feet and turned her firmly to face him. Very gently, he brushed the fingers of one hand across her forehead, so that she could feel the lines of strain being magically soothed away and then, as she closed her eyes, he traced down the frown crease between them.

He lightly tapped the tip of her nose. 'You're working too hard.' When her eyes flew open, he tapped her nose again reprovingly. 'You're pushing yourself, and there really isn't that much hassle to get the job finished.'

But there is, Cam said to herself silently, you just don't understand. However, she merely replied, 'I know, but I enjoy hard work. I don't exactly sit around all day drinking tea at the museum, you know.'

He shook his head, half impatient, half angry. 'Yes, but that's different. I've told you before, out here, you have the heat and the humidity to contend with as well.' He put a finger beneath her chin and, tilting her face towards him, regarded it critically. 'You're looking very tired and strained.'

She didn't need him to tell her that, she thought ruefully. Her mirror told her every morning. But it wasn't, she knew, because of overwork. 'No, really, I'm quite——'

'Be quiet,' he said sternly. 'I will not send you home to your mother,' if he noticed the faint start she gave, he gave no sign, 'ill and exhausted. You've worked for nearly three weeks without a break and you're taking tomorrow off.'

The protests died on her lips. Yes, it would be marvellous to have a whole day off—a day just spent lounging, doing nothing—though not by the pool, she decided rapidly, but on one of the nearby deserted beaches.

'Besides which,' Matt was still speaking, 'you've seen nothing at all of the Cay. You're like one of those tourists who, with all this beauty around them, don't venture further than their hotel gateway.' He hesitated fractionally, then seemed to come to a swift decision. 'I'm going to the other end of the island tomorrow morning, and you're coming with me. No arguments. Oh, and I'll be leaving early—by nine—so make sure you're ready.'

'Sorry I'm late!'

Cam, flustered after her fourth change of outfit since breakfast, hurtled down the steps and threw herself in beside Matt, who was sitting at the wheel of the white open runabout, the engine running. But he merely grunted and contented himself with one ostentatious glance at his watch before putting the vehicle into gear and taking off down the drive.

Cam realised that she was still clutching her beach bag. She tossed it on to the rear seat, then smoothed down her light blue cotton skirt, which after all that agonised indecision—for Matt, apart from telling her to bring her swimming things, had given no clue as to what she should wear—she had matched with a scoop-necked white top.

She sat back, clinging tightly to the sides of her seat, as they swung out on to the winding road. The panic that had flared when Matt had suggested—no, *ordered* her to accompany him this morning had subsided, and, after a restless night, she had accepted that he was right. She was getting tired and jaded, and it was quite true—she hadn't seen anything of the island which, after all, had been her family home for generations.

It did mean, of course, that they would be together in inescapable proximity for hours probably, but yesterday they had worked perfectly amicably, free of the tensions which had so often arisen between them. Perhaps today would seal the beginning of a new, relaxed relationship that would make the rest of her time at Tamarind much more bearable. In any case, she had determined that she was going to enjoy this one stolen day—and Matt seemed to share her resolve, at least to judge from the open, almost boyish grin he shot her as they bounced perilously along the narrow road.

'See those fishing-boats out there?'

He gestured out to sea and, screwing up her eyes against the glare, Cam made out a clutch of rough, single-manned canoes, swarming around the stretch of white water that marked the reef skirting this section of the coast.

'They're from the village where we're heading.'

'What are they fishing for?'

'Well, snapper and crawfish mainly, but they're also after conch, sea urchins, pieces of coral—that sort of thing. I helped Uncle Matt set up an outlet for them. We bought them a pitch in the new St Hilaire craft market. It's only small, but some of the cruise ships are beginning to put in to Port Charlotte, so it should take off. Heaven knows, they need the money, but as Clarence is as proud as the devil, straightforward charity wouldn't work.'

'Clarence?'

'The old chap we're going to see. He was the head

man at Tamarind for years. I've heard that he hasn't
been too well lately. He always refused to retire while
Uncle Matt was still alive, but then I pensioned him off
and now he's the uncrowned king of the village.'

Bellevue village consisted of a dozen or so brightly
painted wood-framed cottages, each with its own small
porch, and was separated from the rough beach only by
a line of coconut palms. As Matt braked sharply by the
furthest house, a gaggle of young boys in khaki shorts
ran from behind it, whooping with joy, and almost
dragged him out of the vehicle.

He greeted them all by name, threw a playful punch
in the direction of each, then shooed them away. He
took out several white-wrapped packages from beside
his seat, then ushered Cam, who was standing hesitantly
beside him, towards the porch steps. Peeping round the
top rail was a toddler, dressed in a spotless white
sundress and hat, and Matt greeted her with a, 'Hi,
Rosalie.'

The child gave him an enchanting, gappy smile, and
when he stooped to swing her up with one arm she
fastened her own plump arms around his neck and
plonked a smacking kiss on his cheek. He set her down
at the bottom of the steps, gave her one of the packages
and shook his finger at her admonishingly.

'Now, these aren't all for you. Make sure you share
them with the others this time.'

On the porch, an elderly man was swinging to and fro
in an old wooden rocker. Matt shook his hand warmly,
introduced Cam, then gave him the rest of the parcels.
She sat back on a wicker chair while the two men talked,
Matt slipping fluently into the lilting patois which she
could not follow. There was a world of age . . . position
. . . circumstances . . . wealth between them, and yet,
she reflected, as she watched them from behind her dark

lenses, there was a perfect easiness and affection between the old and young man.

This was a totally different Matt—one whose existence she would never have suspected. With him seemingly totally engrossed in his conversation, stretched on an ancient swing hammock, she could study him at her ease. How handsome he was. The thin, hard lines of his face were softened for once; the grey eyes, so often wary or downright hostile, had lost their bleakness. As for his body—Cam's eyes flickered momentarily down the old white shorts and navy cotton shirt, open negligently to the waist. The lazy sprawl of his athletic body only enhanced his perfect physique, showing off the long, hard line of his legs, the lean torso, the set of his head . . .

Cam suddenly realised that Matt's eyes were on her. He must have sensed her gaze and, although still talking to Clarence, was watching her in return. She flushed scarlet and hastily removed her eyes to the safety of the floorboards, just as Clarence clapped his hands, and a young woman appeared with three glasses, a bottle of dark gold rum and a Coke on a tray. He poured a very generous tot and looked enquiringly towards Cam, but Matt intervened, shaking his head firmly.

'No, it's too strong for her. She'll just have the Coke.' And, as the two men downed their heady drinks she was left sipping hers in vague resentment—although she had not in the least wanted the rum—and feeling hardly any older than the young boys who were now crawling all over the runabout.

'You remember I told you how one of Uncle Matt's gardeners caught me peeping in at the tapestries when I was a child?' Matt asked her. 'Well, that was Clarence. I was just telling him that you've come to mend them.'

'Oh, yes.' As Cam gave the old man a polite smile, he said something that made Matt laugh out loud.

'He wants to know——' Matt shot her a teasing look, then obviously changed his mind, for although she looked at him questioningly, he set down his empty glass and stood up. 'Come on. Time to go.'

On the floor beside the old man was a gleaming heap of shells and coral. He leaned over, hunted through them, and drew out a beautiful piece of coral, creamy-pink, fan-shaped, with the delicate fronds of a fern. He held it out towards her. 'For you, missy.'

But Cam drew back. It was superb, the pick of the pile, and surely worth a great deal in Port Charlotte market.

'Oh, no——' she began agitatedly, but Matt's hand closed around her arm in a warning squeeze.

'You'd love it, wouldn't you?'

She gave the old man a warm smile. 'Yes—yes, I would. It's beautiful, thank you.'

As they were driving off, Matt said, 'Sorry to leap on you, but remember what I said. They may be poor, but they have a whole lot of pride.'

Cam was giving a last wave to the toddler, who was clutching what remained of Matt's package. 'What a gorgeous little girl. She's Clarence's granddaughter, I suppose.'

'No—his daughter.'

She stared open-mouthed. 'His *daughter*? But—but he must be——'

'Well over seventy. Yes, I know—but out here,' he shot her a look in which there was more than a glint of devilment, 'whether it's the sun, or the heat, or what, the men seem to hang on to their—er—virility almost forever!'

Cam found herself blushing again and as she turned away a sudden feeling of sadness swept through her. Matt's visit was over, they would be back at Tamarind

in under an hour, and there would be most of the
afternoon left. She could even go back to the tapestries.

'Right, you've got your swimsuit?'

'Er—yes. Why, aren't we going back?'

'Back? Of course not.' He sounded almost angry. 'I
told you to take the day off, and that's precisely what
you're doing.'

The road, scarcely more than a track now, wound
through the edge of a banana plantation which rolled
away towards the feet of the hills in the island's interior.
Matt, his eyes firmly on a sharp left-hand bend ahead of
them, remarked conversationally, 'By the way, I had to
correct Clarence on one thing back there.'

Alerted by the frisson of amusement in his voice, she
looked at him enquiringly. 'Oh. What?'

'He wanted to know whether I was following in Uncle
Matt's illustrious footsteps.' He paused. 'You
know—whether I've made you my mistress yet. I had to
put him right.' He swung the wheel dextrously into the
bend. 'Hope you don't mind.'

CHAPTER SIX

AFTER one horrified look, Cam kept her gaze steadfastly on the blue-green line of hills, willing herself not to rise to Matt's bait, but a few minutes later she realised he was pulling off the track. The runabout lurched through some deep ruts, then stopped, and as Matt switched off the engine she was conscious of a loud drumming sound, together with the noise of water splashing.

Just ahead of them was a narrow stone bridge, and when Cam got out and walked on to it she glimpsed, among the huge elephant-eared water plants and green fronds of bamboo, a waterfall. It was cascading down from the hillside above them to disappear under the bridge and then tumble down a series of giant leaps over broad stone ledges towards the sea.

Together they leaned on the low parapet, watching the clear, jade-green water slicing down over the boulders then bursting up into a white spumy spray, while a rainbow arch of moisture hung continuously in the air. Against the roar of water, Matt said something unintelligible, and when she shook her head he gestured towards a steep, overgrown path at the far side of the bridge.

He reached into the runabout, tossed her beach bag at her, then lifted out a wicker basket from the rear seat and led the way down the steep path. She struggled behind him, trying to avoid the sinewy tendrils of creepers which wound themselves everywhere in the moist green shade. Finally, she ducked under the low, spreading branches of an ancient, gnarled cotton tree and emerged into the sunlight.

Matt was just lowering something into the shallow pool at the foot of the fall. When he saw her, he straightened up.

'Like it?'

Cam, rendered totally speechless, nodded. Behind them, the hillside rose steeply in a rippling green semicircle; in front, the sea was a soft, almost pearly green, darkening beyond the reef to inky-blue. The beach, through which the falls had cut a winding channel out to the sea, was a small curve of clotted cream, the sand so fine that when she kicked off her sandals it felt like warm silk.

This is true, heartaching beauty, she thought, and as Matt came up to her she bit her lip. 'It's perfect,' she said simply.

He smiled down at her in complete understanding. 'Yes, it does rather seize you by the throat, doesn't it? I've known this beach since I was a kid, but it still delivers a punch in the midriff every time I come here.'

He hesitated, then added slowly, his eyes on the silver horizon, 'This was always my secret place when I was a boy—I used to cycle here in those days. Sometimes I brought a tent and camped out on the beach. You're the first person I've ever brought here—I've always come alone before.'

There was a bleakness about his half-averted face which moved Cam deeply. 'Thank you, Matt. Thank you for bringing me,' she said huskily, and rested her hand on his arm for a moment in a spontaneous gesture, until, shaking himself free from whatever devils were plaguing him, he smiled at her.

'I'm hot. Fancy a swim before lunch?'

Before she could answer, he had unzipped his shorts to reveal brief black trunks. He shrugged off his shirt, dropped it beside his shorts, then turned and ran off towards the sea. Cam stooped to pick up his discarded clothes then, as she straightened, she froze and they dropped from her hand almost unnoticed . . . His strong, tanned shoulders, the slim waist and tapering hips, emphasised by the one single brief garment he wore, slung low across the top of his thighs . . .

Cam realised that she was staring after him. No, she wasn't—she was feasting her eyes on him. Thankful that his back was safely turned, she hastily picked up his clothes and placed them carefully on to the exposed roots of the cotton tree. In its dense shade, she slipped out of her own clothes and into the green swimsuit, then walked down the beach to wade out into the warm shallows.

Matt was further out, floating lazily on his back though his head was turned in her direction and, suddenly overcome by the fragments of that frighteningly powerful sensation moments before, she rapidly ducked down and struck out through the water. As she splashed nearer to him, he twisted down in one of those swift, eel-like turns and surfaced close beside her, his arm brushing momentarily against her leg.

'Your swimming's improved.'

'Well, I've had plenty of practice lately,' she replied rather breathlessly. But she didn't want to think of all those solitary afternoons in the pool at Tamarind, so she said quickly, 'Race you to that log.'

He looked at the log, low in the water and drifting idly in the current about thirty yards away. 'OK, off you go.'

When Cam had covered almost half the distance, she risked a quick glance over her shoulder. Matt was only just unhurriedly launching himself. Huh, so he thought he could beat her with both hands tied behind his back, did he? She'd show him, though exactly why it was so important to show him she didn't know.

She threw herself through the water, spluttering as a little wave smacked at her face, every fibre straining towards that piece of bobbing driftwood. As Matt came up alongside her, she hurled herself at the log, her fingers dragging against its sodden bark.

'I won!' she shouted triumphantly.

'You sure did.' He was grinning at her and, at the open amusement in his eyes her smile turned to a scowl.

'You let me win.'

He shook his head. 'Now, would I do that?'

'Yes, you would.'

'Uh-uh. Scout's honour.'

She eyed him doubtfully. '*Were* you a boy scout?'

'Afraid not. But anyway, you're certainly coming on—and you're not even bothered,' he added casually, 'about being out in fifteen feet of water.'

'What?'

Cam looked down. Far below—way past her toes, it seemed—little ripples of sand stirred on the sea bed. She threw a glance towards the shore. The beach looked miles away, the picnic basket a child-sized toy. As she clutched the log, it lurched then settled itself lower into the water. She gave a strangled gasp, loosed it and, quite panic-stricken, grabbed at Matt. They both went under, then came up spluttering, his hands under her elbows as he hoisted her up. He supported her until she stopped choking, then fixed her with his eyes.

'Tell me, Cam, just why, whenever you get near me in water, do you have this compulsive urge to drown me?'

In reply, she could manage no more than an uncertain, bleary-eyed smile. Was he trying obliquely to remind her of that first afternoon, that kiss in the pool, or did his very casualness show that that episode, so swiftly over, had been carelessly dismissed from his mind? She couldn't tell—and didn't know which she wanted it to be.

He propelled her away from the log. 'Come on. I'll tow you in.'

'No—no, I can manage. I'll swim back,' she blurted out, and kicked for the shore.

Back on the beach, she dropped on to her front on the warm sand, her head propped on her folded arms, and from the shelter of her wide-brimmed pink cotton sunhat watched that sleek black head moving purposefully towards her. As he waded out, though, she closed her eyes, feigning sleep. His footsteps crunched and a moment later she felt a shower of water droplets prickle on her hot skin and heard him flop down on the sand. She opened her eyes cautiously, then saw that he too had sprawled out on his front. His head was propped on his cupped hands and he was watching her, his eyes inches from hers, an enigmatic expression in them.

But all he said was, 'So you like my beach?'

Cam's eyes slid gratefully away from his. 'Oh, yes,' she exclaimed in unfeigned enthusiasm. 'I'd come here every day if——'

She broke off and he prompted her, his brows raised questioningly. 'If?'

'I—I was only going to say,' she began again, reluctantly, 'if I lived here.'

He studied her for a moment, then said abruptly, 'Do you drive?'

She looked at him, startled. 'Yes, I passed my test last year.'

'Well, then—feel free to borrow the runabout and

come here whenever you want.'

'Oh, no, I couldn't possibly.'

'Why not?'

Because if you weren't here, it wouldn't be the same, she almost said, but instead, forcing this unnerving thought from her, she managed to smile. 'I don't think it would take too much to turn me into a permanent lotus-eater, and then what would happen to your tapestries?'

'Oh, of course, we mustn't forget the tapestries, must we?' There was no mistaking the undercurrent of ironic amusement in his voice, but then he went on, 'So you think I did the right thing, not selling out to Brannan International for a fast buck?'

She stared at him. 'Brannan International—the hotel chain?'

He nodded. 'Yes. They got their fingers badly burned a couple of years back over a beach site on St Hilaire,' he smiled in some private reminiscence, 'and then, almost before Uncle Matt was dead,' his voice hardened, 'they were trying it here. At first they wanted me to sell them the whole of Halcyon Cay, and then, when that was no dice, they came back again, with plans for an upmarket hotel complex for the ultra-rich right here.'

'What did you say?'

'I told them politely—well, *fairly* politely, that as long as I'm around, no one lays a finger on this place, or anywhere else on the entire Cay.'

Cam realised that she had been holding her breath and now she let it out in a gasp of pure relief. To have all this tranquil natural beauty ravaged—it was too awful to contemplate. And yet, wait a minute. What a sentimental fool she was. Surely it would be better to have this beach—the whole Cay—in the impersonal if greedy hands of anonymous strangers, rather than as the illicit booty of an endless line of Corrigans—Matt's children, then their children . . .

'What's the matter?' The present Corrigan was watching her intently.

'I—oh, nothing.' Terrified that his razor-sharp mind might penetrate her thoughts, she sat up abruptly, busying herself with trying to brush the tacky sand from her arms and legs.

Matt sat back on his haunches then got up, and held his hands out to her. 'You'll never get it off that way. Come on, I'll show you.'

He pulled her to her feet and led her, still keeping a casual hold of her hand, to where the stream met the sea. At first, as they splashed along, the water had all the gentle warmth of the sun-filled sea, then gradually, as the salt and fresh waters mingled, it became colder, until in the pool immediately below the fall it had an exhilarating chill.

'When I was a kid, I used to try to find the exact point where the two waters met, then lie there, so that my top half was warm and my legs were cold.'

His words conjured up an idyllic childhood—the idyllic childhood she should have had, Cam thought, and yet there was no bitterness in her heart towards him because, for some reason which she could not fathom, all that he had said of his upbringing and of this place somehow engendered in her a picture, not of carefree enjoyment, but of a lonely, even unhappy childhood.

But she didn't want to begin to feel sorry for Matt—and he certainly wouldn't thank her if she did—so she bent down and started scooping up handfuls of water to splash over herself, while he went back to the wicker box and knelt beside it.

Above her, that series of shallow steps stretched back

invitingly towards the bridge. She began to scramble up from one rock-ledge to another, the green, shadow-dappled water foaming round her ankles, or occasionally up to her knees. She was about half-way up when, from below, she heard Matt call her. He was standing directly at the foot of the falls, a camera in his hand. He pointed towards it and Cam called, 'Oh, sorry—I'll get out of the way.'

But he gestured impatiently to her and yelled back, 'No. Stay right where you are.'

She stood self-consciously, looking down at him as he took two or three shots from different angles. Then, holding the camera carefully, he climbed up several of the ledges towards her before stopping and pointing imperiously to a small, extremely uncomfortable-looking cushion of rock in mid-stream. She perched precariously on its chill surface; there was a snag on the stone—she could feel it and it would catch her swimsuit.

Surreptitiously, she eased one buttock forward and Matt shouted, 'Keep still—and shake your hair forward!'

She dragged her fingers through her hair obediently and held herself steady as he took his shot.

'Right. Just one more.'

He moved fractionally to his left and crouched low, but this time, on a sudden impulse of mischief, just as she sensed that he was about to release the shutter, she wrinkled her nose and pulled a face at him. Matt did not say anything, but merely lowered the camera and stared up at her for an instant. Very deliberately, he set down the camera on a safe ledge, then suddenly he swung round and sprang with lightning speed up on to the next shelf of rock.

At the expression on his face, Cam, with a yelp of terror, leapt to her feet and fled up the falls, scrambling from rock to rock with total disregard for her hands and toes. Under the bridge she almost slipped, righted herself, then hesitated. If he were to slip, he could badly hurt his already damaged knee. She couldn't hear him—perhaps he'd already fallen and was lying helpless at the foot of the falls.

But, even as she pulled up abruptly, Matt, with a cry of triumph, had wound his arms round her and was clasping her to him so tightly that she was aware of the whole lean length of his body and could feel the surge of his heart beating against her skin. He turned her round, his face lit by the dancing reflections from the stone bridge just above their heads. He was laughing down at her, but then suddenly the smile faded and he was looking at her with an expression which she had never seen on his face before, a look of surprise—no, *shock*, which made her insides flutter butterfly-like with nervous tremulousness.

'Cam?'

There was a question in his voice. His hands tightened their grip on her arms, drawing her almost imperceptibly towards him. He was going to kiss her and, despite all her vows, she would not resist him. Her own lips were already parting, her eyes closing, when she felt him draw a deep breath, then give her a quick shake before saying brusquely, 'Time for lunch—I'm starving,' and almost before she could register that he had dropped his hold on her, as though the touch of her flesh was burning hot, he had turned and was leaping from rock to rock back down the cascade.

Cam leaned against the supports of the bridge for a few moments, watching until he disappeared from sight. The only reminder that he had been holding her seconds before was the soft prickling of the tiny gold hairs on her upper arms, crushed under the fierceness of his grip, and a curious sense, not exactly of sadness, but of sharp, almost physical deflation which was welling inside her.

But then she shook herself free of this depressing feeling. Matt was quite right: it was she who was being foolish. He was sensibly—no, *considerately*, keeping to their unspoken resolution, and was determinedly preventing any tensions from intruding to spoil their—or rather her day. By taking her out—above all, bringing her here, to what was clearly for him such a special place—it was as though he was giving her today as a gift, which she could remember always, perfect and unclouded, and she was intensely grateful to him for that . . . Slowly, she followed him down to the beach.

The hamper was open, Matt on his knees beside it, piling two plates with chicken slices from an insulated coldbox. As she approached, he looked up. 'Pâté?' His tone was perfectly normal.

'Yes, please.'

She sat down, relieved that her voice betrayed nothing of the tumultuous feelings which had swept through her moments before.

'Can you get the wine?' He gestured towards the pool where, wedged securely under its sandy rim, she found a bottle of white wine, achingly chill against her hands.

It was a delightful, leisurely meal. Cam could not remember when she had enjoyed a meal as much—never, she decided finally. They ate in the shade of the cotton tree, leaning side by side against its trunk, as Matt brought out a seemingly endless supply of food; thin rolled slices of ham and rare roast beef, a delicious cheese custard in a melting flaky pastry case, salads, spicy avocado dip, crusty french loaves, butter and cheeses.

Finally, he split two large mangoes and removed the

stones, their pearly flesh running juice all over his hands, then fished out a carton of strawberries from the cold box.

'I didn't know strawberries grew out here,' Cam exclaimed, watching as he tipped some into the hollow of each mango.

'They don't grow at sea-level, of course, but years ago Uncle Matt set up a smallholding in the hills up there. It gives work for several families, and provides us with strawberries, raspberries, even peaches when the season isn't too dry. The cherry trees failed, though. Pity—I could have fed you with them.'

He handed her a plate, piled with the scented, glossy fruit, then raised his wineglass. 'Here's to you, Cam—and may you get your heart's desire, whatever that may be.'

Just for a moment, that thread of tension which had been present so often twanged almost perceptibly between them, then Cam raised her glass in turn. 'And to you, Matt.'

When they had at last finished she repacked the hamper, while he lay on his back in the shade, one hand flung behind his head, his last glass of wine balanced carefully on his tanned stomach. She knew he was watching her through the crook of his arm, but she did not turn round until she had finished, and then she saw that his eyes had closed. Very gently, she lifted the almost empty glass out of his curled hand and put it away, then she too, drowsy with wine, rich food and languorous heat, stretched out in the shade of the tree . . .

When they woke, it was late afternoon and the tree was already casting long black fingers of shadow across the beach. They swam again, but this time Matt obviously intended to be on his own. As she came towards him, he suddenly turned and began swimming hard away from her, apparently going hell for leather for the reef. For a moment she felt again that same touch of sadness, but again she shook herself free of it—after all, she already knew how moody, not to say mercurial, his temperament was.

When he eventually returned, shaking the water out of his hair, he went to stand under the spray from the waterfall, rinsing the salt vigorously from his body. On an impulse, Cam fetched out her camera from her beach bag. As she approached, he looked up, then scowled when he saw the camera, but too late.

'Smile, please,' she called sweetly, and before he could retreat she had caught him perfectly, framed against the falls and an overhanging tree.

As she lowered the camera, she thought, quite dispassionately, I shall always remember this moment: the falls, the trees, the roar of water—and Matt. His image blurred suddenly, and she hastily bent her head to wind on the film.

When he finally emerged, she held out the camera. 'Will you take one of me, please?' With an effort, she kept her expression blank, apart from a wry smile. 'Next winter, when all this is like an impossible dream, I shall want to be reminded of today.'

He took the shot, then handed the camera back to her. 'Your film's finished, I think.'

She looked down at it. 'Yes, it is.' She had already used most of the film, rather surreptitiously, on shots of Tamarind, mainly thinking of her mother. 'Do you get your films developed on St Hilaire, or do you have to send them to the States?'

'Neither. I can develop them for you, if you like. I've got my own darkroom at the house.'

'Oh, I didn't realise. You take it quite seriously, then—photography, I mean?'

'Yes, you could say that,' he replied briefly, and then looked up at the sky. 'It'll be dark soon. Time to go, I'm afraid.'

They drew up outside Tamarind as a molten-red sunset flared on their faces and turned the façade of the house to peach-pink. As he cut the engine, she turned to him impulsively. 'Thank you, Matt. It's been marvellous.'

He looked at her for what seemed a long time, his expression hidden in the shadow of his drill sunhat; then, very gently, he took hold of the hand which was nearer to him and, raising it, softly kissed the palm. She tried not to tremble under his touch but, though he must have felt the tremor run through her, he only said, 'My pleasure.'

In bed that night, Cam retraced every minute detail of the day. It had been a truly unforgettable day—and Matt had made it. But what would tomorrow bring? She didn't know, and dared not look into her mind to try to see there what she wanted the future to give her. All she would allow herself was the certainty that, when morning came, she would be with Matt once more.

But in the morning, Matt was nowhere to be seen. Breakfast and lunch were both, once again, solitary meals. Although she could not bring herself to ask, Miss Poppy told her that he had gone off on business and would be away all day, so she remained alone in the tapestry salon, completing the cleaning that they had worked at together.

Then, when she had gone upstairs to get ready for dinner—still not sure whether he would be joining her or not—she heard his voice in the hall. Her hand was poised on her bedroom door, and for a moment she had to fight the compulsive urge to run back downstairs on some flimsy pretext. But instead she went on into the room, shutting the door quietly behind her.

She showered, then went through to the bedroom and opened her wardrobe door. Normally she dressed quite simply for dinner, but this evening it suddenly seemed to her imperative that she should look her absolute best. As she flicked along the row of clothes, though, her heart sank. If only she'd bothered more back home. Well, it would just have to be the grey and white cotton shirt-dress she'd worn on the first evening.

But then, as she was pulling it out, she caught sight of a dress right at the back of the wardrobe, where it had hung neglected since her arrival. It was the one that her mother had pressed on her, coming in just as she'd finished packing. 'Do take it, darling. Your clothes sense is so awful,' here Mrs Lucas had shaken her head in exasperated despair, 'and you might be glad of it.' And so, touched by her mother's gesture, which she knew she could ill afford, Cam had stifled her protests.

Now, she slowly drew it out, her heart beating just a little faster. She slipped it on, tied the narrow, rolled belt tightly and bloused out the soft, silk chiffon folds of the bodice over it. She moved a little and saw in the mirror how the soft, unpressed pleats of the skirt rippled around her, how the scoop of the neckline revealed her shadowed breasts, and how the dark, ripe-damsom shade enhanced her hair, her fair colouring, now tanned to a delicate gold, and, as she stared disbelievingly at herself, the soft, intense depths of her violet eyes.

Instead of pinning her hair up, she combed it through, then left it to hang in shining blonde silk strands, just caught up behind her ears with slides. She only had one lipstick, a soft pink gloss, but fortunately it went happily with the deep tone of her dress. Her dark brown mascara was so ancient that she had to wet it under the tap to unclog it, but then two coats brought her eyes sharply into focus. Those eyes . . . Cam stared thoughtfully into her own irises. She must be careful. They had an altogether new, tender, dark velvety softness which, to Matt's penetrating gaze, might very well betray her . . .

He was standing on the veranda, leaning his elbow against one of the uprights, his back to her. He had not seen her, but there was a forbidding quality about that back which made her suddenly hesitant. As she hung indecisively in the open doorway, one nervous hand pleating her neckline, he must somehow have sensed her behind him, for he swung round.

His eyes swiftly raked over her, taking in the dress, the line of her body through it, the swell of her breasts, then finally came to rest, quite expressionless, on her face. Total silence hung, almost visible, between them for a few instants, then he muttered a bare greeting and held up his own empty glass.

'Drink?'

Cam, repelled and shocked by the chill formality of his manner, bit her lip. Was this the light-hearted, teasing companion of yesterday? Surely, no—surely this hard-faced, cold-eyed man was a total stranger? And yet, in the end, surely this was the real Matt Corrigan? Perhaps yesterday he had somehow sensed her growing feelings for him, and now, far from the softening influence of that lonely beach, he was warning her off, erecting once more that 'no entry' sign around the territory of his private self.

'I said, do you want a drink?'

There was more than a hint of impatience in his voice and she said quickly, 'N-no, thank you.'

He nodded briefly, then brushed past her. She crossed

the polished wood floor and stood gazing sightlessly out into the warm, rustling night. Behind her, she heard the clink of glass as he poured himself another drink, but he did not rejoin her, and when Miss Poppy called her to the table he was already in his place.

All the while the servants were around, he made no effort to keep up even a limping pretence at conversation. Cam waded through the delicious food as if it were old potato peelings and, judging from his expression when she shot him the occasional sliding, sidelong glance, he thought exactly the same.

By the end of the meal, Cam wanted nothing more than to run away and hide herself, but when the maid carried through the tray of coffee, pride forced her to her feet and out on to the veranda again. As she mechanically raised and set down her cup, Matt toyed moodily with the sugar crystals in the bowl, until her over-tautened nerves jangled almost audibly. When he at last threw down the spoon, she jumped.

'I'm off to New York in the morning.'

'Oh?' This was all the response that she could trust herself to make.

'I was wondering if——' He broke off, seemed to hesitate for a moment, then went on brusquely, 'Do you need anything—for your work, I mean? Halcyon Cay, and St Hilaire, come to that, aren't exactly over-endowed with tapestry repair materials.'

'Oh, no—no, thank you,' she replied quickly. 'I've brought everything I want from London.'

He nodded acquiescence, put down his cup and uncoiled himself swiftly from his chair. 'In that case, if you'll excuse me, I need to pack.'

Cam stared up at him. He hadn't said one word about how long he would be away. A week? A month? A year? But, though she ached to know, she would not—

she *would* not give him the satisfaction of asking. So, when he nodded briefly to her again, she merely gave him a faint smile and a wooden, 'Have a good trip.'

CHAPTER SEVEN

IN THE MORNING, as soon as she woke, Cam felt the emptiness in the house, and did not need Miss Poppy to tell her that Mr Corrigan had already left. A leaden heaviness had settled on Tamarind and on her, so that all she wanted to do was to moon listlessly about. Instead, though, she once again tried to immerse herself in the tapestries. But she, who had always been, even as a child, totally self-sufficient, able to absorb herself contentedly in her work, would over and over shake herself awake from an unhappy daydream to find herself frowning intently at the same half-completed clump of woven primroses.

Time and again, the bitter-sweet memories would rise up in her consciousness: the touch of his lips in the pool, the brush of his fingers against her cheek and, above all, every moment of their magical stolen day. But each time she would thrust them fiercely from her. Matt, however brutally he had set about it, was right—he knew, and she must accept, that for her any relationship with him must be wholly self-destructive . . .

One morning, she was alone as usual, sitting cross-legged on the floor of the salon, her lap filled with those same primroses, as she worked with methodical neatness, forming tiny diagonal stitches across each rent in the fabric, the slippery needle squeaking slightly at each stitch. As she wiped her hot palms, her eyes strayed past the pale yellow flowers to the celandines, the white anemones. The artist had captured in a few

97

square inches all the flowers of an English spring—wood violets, pansies . . . 'Soft violet eyes, but they darken to pansy purple when you're angry, I see. Though I wonder what entrancing shade they might be, if someone . . .'

Cam pushed the stiff, heavy folds of cloth from her lap and scrambled precipitately to her feet. The room was suddenly smothering, claustrophobic, and she had to get out.

She hurried outdoors to the small yard where, the previous evening, she had hung up to dry her latest experiment in mixing vegetable dyes. But when she reached the line where the hanks of yarn were hanging, she saw at once that this attempt, too, was a failure. What had seemed yesterday when wet to be the perfect match was now still not the delicate pink of the wild-rose garland in Europa's golden hair, but merely a modern lipstick-pink.

Cam stamped her foot. The frustration which had been simmering in her for several days at last boiled over and, with an angry gesture, she tore the yarn from the line, splitting the pegs in half. A total waste of time! She would have to begin yet again that evening. Then, as she stuffed the yarn into her bag, she realised with horrified amazement that her eyes were scalding with tears. Next moment, she was crying quite uncontrollably, but then, hearing the voices of the gardeners and their approaching footsteps, she fumbled out her handkerchief, hastily mopped her wet face, and somehow choked down her heaving sobs.

Just what was wrong with her now? she asked herself as she wearily climbed the stairs to her room. Getting in such a state, when it was only a matter of time before she got it right. And besides, this was normally one of the challenging aspects of her work that she most enjoyed. She would not allow herself to be upset over it any longer—she would have another attempt later . . .

That afternoon, though, when even her swim had failed to erase totally the feeling that she was being slowly suffocated, she wandered around the extensive grounds that lay between the rear of the house and the plantations. Hidden behind a neglected, overgrown hedge, she found a small, secluded garden, clearly long-abandoned. Its narrow gravelled paths had all but disappeared under a riot of tropical growth, and she had to push her way through stiff-stemmed shrubs, which gave off a pungent, bitter smell as she brushed against them, to where, at the end of a slight rise, she discovered a broken seat under a tangle of white-starred frangipani.

She perched precariously on it, drinking in the sweetness of the perfume and gazing out over the foliage that swirled around her, to break like a green sea at the foot of the hedge which bounded the garden on all sides. As she stared listlessly at it, some kind of broken pattern gradually took shape in front of her, until she drew in her breath in a gasp of astonishment. Surely? And yet it couldn't be—not here. But yes, those lines which under her now eager eye formed themselves into a huge square, those cool, formal curves . . . She was looking at an English knot garden, neglected perhaps for a hundred years, but a knot none the less. Of course—those bushes which she had had to push her way through, and that so-familiar smell, which she had not recognised, simply because she had not expected to find it here, was the sharp, peppery scent of box leaves.

Cam sat frowning. The stylised, symmetrical lines of knot gardens had been out of fashion for centuries, so who could have planted this one, so far from England?

The answer came swiftly. Richard Forrester, the original Puritan owner of Tamarind, whom Matt had accused of being all kinds of hypocrite and unscrupulous villain. She gave an involuntary half-smile. What had he said of him—seduced by the sun and the tropics? Maybe so, but he must also have missed the native land he would never dare to return to—and so he had constructed here a small, quintessentially English garden.

And yet, just as he had succumbed to the overpowering influence of his new world, so his garden too had yielded to the inexorable advance of the tropics. The box hedges themselves, originally closely manicured to a height of a foot or less, now towered above Cam, while through their close-knit branches cascaded torrents of red, purple and pink bougainvillaea, interwoven with exotic tree orchids. There was a huge one, its flowering stems stirring in the slight breeze just above her head like some snaky-haired Medusa. Cam shuddered. She felt all around her a pulsating life force, vivid, insatiable. Could nothing hope to withstand its gentle violence, she thought with a sudden twinge of panic.

Over in one corner was an enormous poinsettia—six month red, six month green, as one of Matt's gardeners had called it—bearing its brilliant scarlet leaves on stems ten feet tall. Last Christmas she had given her mother a small one in a pot, which she had bought from a barrow boy near the museum. Though it had promptly died on them, she could still remember the sense of exuberant tropical warmth which it had brought to their faded living-room.

At the memory of that room, the house, the quiet back streeet, hot tears stung her eyes and she rested her chin on her fists, staring miserably at the ground. Oh, why had she ever come to Tamarind? Just a few unsuspecting hours in a jet, and her calm, ordered, uneventful existence had been destroyed for ever, for she knew suddenly, with a dreadful certainty, that however thoroughly she might, once this task was over, settle back into the quiet, regular sameness of home and job, she herself, like her Puritan forebear—and his garden—had, under the subtle, insidious influences of her surroundings, changed irrevocably.

But was it, after all, the island that was to blame? Cam sat very still, the colour seeping from her face. She had deluded herself utterly when she had insisted that all that mattered was the successful completion of her assignment, that all that she would then have to do was pack her bags and walk up the aircraft steps, leaving Tamarind and Halcyon Cay behind without the faintest sense of loss. Even if she fled now, today, taking the next flight home—or anywhere, so long as it was away from here—nothing could ever be wholly the same again.

One kiss, one fleeting caress, one single day—that was all it had been. And yet, here she was, counting the minutes, almost the seconds, until Matt returned. Cam gave a rueful smile. Was she, at the ripe-old age of twenty-four, suffering the equivalent of a first teenage crush? Were her feelings for Matt Corrigan no more, in the final analysis, than the hopeless worship of the latest pop idol? She seemed, after all, to be showing much the same starry-eyed, symptoms! But, no, Cam thought suddenly, and quite matter-of-factly. Of course, what a fool, what a blind fool I've been. I love him.

But since when? Had love sneaked up on her, unnoticed, on one of those silent evenings sitting opposite him at dinner, or on that deserted sun-filled beach? No, not then. And not even on that first afternoon by the pool. She had been blind for too long, but now the scales were falling from her eyes with a vengeance. She had loved him from the very beginning. The damage had been done, the mischief set working in her, like some slow-acting drug, on that first intoxicating, wave-buffeting ride out to the Cay. But the knowledge gave her no pleasure now, only an empty, sinking feeling which was akin to panic . . .

Very near her, a cricket, dazed into torpor by the afternoon heat, had began to chirrup again and the sun was slanting long shadows across the garden. She glanced at her watch. Matt had been away now for six days and eight—no, nine hours. Perhaps he would come tomorrow, on the direct evening flight from New York. Oh, Matt, come back tomorrow! Cam closed her eyes momentarily, fiercely willing him with all the force of her being to be on that plane . . .

She slipped in through the side door, the passage dim and cool after the burning heat of the garden. A narrow back staircase led to the bedrooms; she put her foot on the first stair, then stopped as she heard rapid footsteps. Someone was coming down the stairs, was turning the last bend towards her, but after the dazzling sunlight she could not quite see . . .

Matt checked abruptly when he saw her, then, as Cam stared up at him, frozen, he slowly descended the last few stairs. He was here. Back in the garden, she had willed him to return—and here he was: bare-footed, dressed only in swimming-trunks, and with a towel hitched casually over one bronzed shoulder. Through some totally unsuspected supernatural power, she had conjured him up!

A wild desire to laugh welled crazily inside her for an instant, then died away, to be replaced by a terrible, aching longing to touch him, to hold him, a longing so powerful that she felt her hands begin to move towards him as though they had been endowed with life of their own, and she had to thrust them hard into the pockets of her sundress.

His face, as he stood looking down at her, was in deep shadow so that she could not see his expression. But she sensed that he was frowning down at her unsmilingly, and the wave of sheer rapture that had been breaking through her died before the instinctive, radiant smile reached her lips. That barrier of cool reserve that had lain between them before Matt's departure was still there, she realised, its strength, if anything, increased by their days apart.

At last, he broke the silence. 'I was coming to look for you,' he said brusquely. 'I thought you might like a swim.'

'Oh, no—I've already bathed,' she responded quickly. 'Actually, I—I was just going back to work.'

'But of course. Work.' A sardonic smile fleetingly crossed his face. 'Don't let me detain you.'

He gave a dismissive gesture, but she hesitated, unwilling in spite of herself to turn away from him. 'I—I didn't think the New York flight got in until five-thirty.'

'It doesn't,' he replied briefly, then added, with obvious reluctance, 'I finished what I had to do, and didn't feel like hanging around, so,' he shrugged, 'I hired a private jet this morning.'

'I see,' said Cam slowly. What a bundle of complex energies this man was; so impatient that he could not wait a few short hours for a plane, but driven compulsively by some inner demon, he had——

Without warning, Matt stepped down to her level, so that in the narrow stairwell they were very close—

too close. Cam drew back against the wall, but she could still feel his warm breath on her face, see the sheen of dark hair on his chest, even discern faintly the beat of his heart against the smooth, tanned skin. All at once, her mouth felt very dry and she ran her tongue round her lips. But, before she could speak, from far away a telephone shrilled loudly, making them both start.

Matt swore forcibly and ran his fingers through his hair. 'I've already had one long call since I got back, and I'm not in the mood for another. If Miss Poppy finds you, tell her you haven't seen me, and no, I'm not in the pool.'

He eased past her and disappeared, the soft crunch of his footsteps on the gravel path fading behind him.

Cam went slowly upstairs, showered and washed her hair, still tacky from the pool, but then, instead of returning to the salon, she opened the louvres in her pretty sitting-room and hunched on the wide window-sill, hugging her knees to her chin and staring out across the foaming tips of the palms to the narrow ribbon of sea and beyond that, the sky, almost lost in a shimmering haze.

'I love Matt.' She had not realised that she had spoken aloud until she heard the words, and then she looked guiltily over her shoulder, as if half expecting to see someone behind her. 'I love him,' she said again to a green lizard that was sunning itself on a branch of the poinciana tree which overhung the room, but there was no joy in saying it—only a forlorn sadness, a heavy ache which had already broken out all over her body and was now busy centralising itself into a solid lump of pain around her third rib.

So this is how it feels, she thought bleakly—those pangs of unrequited love that her favourite poets were so fond of wallowing in. Matt had accused her of leading a pampered, sheltered life. Well, however sheltered and vicarious her existence might have been until now, she was certainly finding out at first hand what life was all about. She was paying now for her folly and, what was even worse, she knew with a frightening clarity that what she felt now was a mere token of the suffering which still awaited her.

Somehow, though, she had to bear it, and somehow—she set her soft mouth into a thin, drawn-out line—she *would* bear it. In the meantime, she must see Matt as seldom as possible, be as cool as possible when she did—no great problem, after all, for his attitude had been chillingly offhand before he had left and, from their hurried encounter just now, there was no sign of it being any different now he had returned—get through the work as quickly as possible, and then leave Tamarind for ever. She would find no solace while she was here. The mending of a badly damaged heart could only begin once Halcyon Cay had dipped away beneath the plane's wings.

Cam closed her eyes, butting her chin hard against her knees. Oh, if only she could leave now. But perhaps she could. She could pretend her mother was ill. Yes, that was it. She could tell Matt at dinner; he might be—no, *would* be angry—but he would surely not attempt to prevent her leaving in those circumstances—he might even be pleased to see her go.

As for her curious colleagues, she could manufacture some story for them . . . The climate—yes . . . Halcyon Cay, the West Indies, had not agreed with her at all . . . And that was true, if the rest was a farrago of lies, she thought unhappily. Maybe lushly beautiful tropical islands should only be available on doctors' prescriptions—and then only with a government health edict: 'Warning: too much tropical moonlight can severely damage your heart.'

On the other hand, flight would be the easy, the coward's way out. What was it people said? That we've all got one acting role in us? Well then, let this be the performance of Cam Lucas's life. And yet, to see Matt a dozen times a day, to feel this pain intensifying itself a notch at a time as though she was being racked—how could she endure it?

A flock of small sea birds wheeled over the house, their snowy whiteness turned to rose pink by the low sun. She uncurled herself and went to get ready for dinner.

The meal passed in virtual silence. Matt had gathered that impenetrable cloak of cold reserve around him once more, and whenever Cam stole a furtive look from under her lashes he was frowning down darkly at the table. It was, she thought bleakly, as though he had never been away.

She was toying desultorily with her lime sorbet when he suddenly spoke, jolting her out of her unhappy thoughts. 'How's the work progressing?'

'Oh, fine, on the whole. The only problem is——' She stopped, deciding too late that it would have been better to say nothing.

Matt frowned. 'Yes?' he prompted impatiently. 'The only problem——?'

'Well, it's nothing, really,' she went on reluctantly. 'It's just that I'm having difficulty matching up a couple of the shades. I've had several sessions with the dyes, but I don't seem able——'

'These dyes—would they have been available in New York?'

'Well,' she prevaricated, 'I—I expect so.'

He set down his wineglass with a bang, completely

shattering the fragile stem under the weight of his hand, then threw it on to the table.

'I asked you,' he said in a dangerously quiet voice, 'I asked you before I left if there was anything you wanted me to get you. But no, you were quite sure you had everything you needed.'

Cam, feeling her stomach tightening into a hard knot of misery, tried to meet his angry eyes but failed. Looking down at her plate, she swallowed. 'I—I'm sorry.'

'Sorry?' Matt began, but then, as the maid came through with a tray of coffee, he fell silent, morosely flicking his dessert spoon up and down against the Minton plate. 'Thank you, Colette, you can clear away later.' He smiled at the maid as she returned from putting the coffee on the veranda, then waited until she had gone before gracing Cam with another scowl. 'Why didn't you ask me—are you stupid or something?'

When she did not reply, he thrust back his chair savagely, so that it fell with a crash, and went across to the side table to pour himself a brandy. Without turning back to her, he demanded, 'Well? I'm waiting for an answer.'

'I th-thought I'd have all the shades I needed—or at least be able to mix them. I'm sure it'll come right. I'll try again tomorrow.'

Matt swung round to face her. 'So it seems I was right, after all. I'm not at all sure I should let you try again tomorrow,' his voice was a savage imitation of the tone she had used, 'or even let you loose on those tapestries again. It's simply not worth the risk of having those superb works of art ruined by some bungling, inefficient——'

Cam gasped and put a hand to her mouth as though he had struck her. He was being so unreasonable, his reaction so violent to what was really quite a trivial matter. She *would* get the shades right, she knew she would, given time—but it looked as though Matt was not prepared to give her that time. She could feel the treacherous tears welling up in her again. Just a few hours ago she had been longing for his return, aching for him to be with her again, and now—now that he had come, the joy of his return had been brutally destroyed. He was being so unfair, so cruel.

She'd been right all along. There *was* cruelty lurking just beneath the surface of that saturnine countenance, and it was now being unleashed, with terrifying ferocity, on her. But still, somehow, she must hold on to her pride, must sit here unflinching as he hurled these deliberate, wounding barbs at her. And at least, she thought, with a twist of scaffold humour, Matt was making it easier by the minute for her to leave Tamarind the next morning—and this, she knew suddenly, was what she intended to do. She would go upstairs and pack later, but first she must get through the rest of what had suddenly become a nightmare confrontation.

She clenched her hands tightly together in her lap so that her whitened knuckles brushed against the soft folds of her dress.

'If you say so,' she said woodenly. Later, she would resent his wholly unreasonable anger, but not now. Now, she was only capable of feeling a dead despair which, perhaps mercifully, was numbing all other sensations.

'You really are a novice, aren't you? In fact, totally inexperienced in every way.'

Cam leapt to her feet, her chair tottering behind her. Feeling her face crumple even as she moved, she swung round to escape, but she heard Miss Poppy's voice just outside, and instead, in a blind frenzy to be free of his scathing taunts, she flung herself wildly across the room, along the veranda and down the steps into the protecting night.

CHAPTER EIGHT

BESIDE the entrance to the pool, Cam slowed. But no, she must hide herself more securely from inquisitive eyes before she indulged this terrible need to cry which was growing on her second by second. Of their own volition now, her feet were carrying her towards the old, neglected garden. In the pale moonlight, she ducked through the overgrown hedge, to stumble along the paths, falling on all fours once as a creeper caught at her foot, then into the scented bower where she could huddle down on to the broken seat and give herself over at last to her tears . . .

She hardly registered the footsteps crunching on the gravel, as someone felt their unaccustomed way through the garden; only when that someone also tripped and began cursing fluently did Cam still suddenly. Catching back the half-formed sob and straining her eyes and ears, she shrank into the dense shadows cast by the overhanging shrubs.

A moment later, Matt was standing over her at the mouth of the arbour. For a second they stared at one another, each face a pale blur in the blue-white tropical moonlight, then, as Cam made an instinctive movement away from him, he crossed the ground between them in two strides and perched himself precariously beside her.

He was carrying something—a book—but he threw this down on the ground, then put his hand under her chin and firmly, though with the utmost gentleness, turned her face to his. He lifted his other hand as though to stroke her cheek, then, obviously feeling the tears, gave an angry, incoherent exclamation. Next moment he had gathered her to him in a fierce, totally irresistible embrace, one hand encircling her back, the other pressing her head tight against his chest. He laid his cheek against the top of her head, rocking her softly.

'Cam, I'm sorry.' His voice was a whisper against her hair.

'It's—it's all right.'

'But it isn't,' he said savagely. 'I shouldn't have said those dreadful things.'

'No, you were quite right,' she began. 'The dyes——'

'To hell with the bloody dyes—and the bloody tapestries, too! I shouldn't have reacted like that. It's just that—I was almost crazy to get back here. I've been like a cat on hot bricks all the time I've been away. And then, when I did get back, you seemed so—cool, so unwelcoming, not even remotely pleased to see me.'

Holding her away from him, he shot her the pallid ghost of a wry smile. 'Well, say something, for heaven's sake, Cam. Don't just stare at me with those lovely eyes still blurred with the tears I've made you shed.'

Cam's heart was beginning to beat in erratic bounds and she stared at him in silent bewilderment.

'Suddenly, this morning, I knew I couldn't wait, not even for the afternoon flight. I had to get back here—you were like a fever in my mind, my blood. But even then it wasn't until, calling myself all kinds of fool, I was twenty thousand feet up above the Caribbean, that it hit me square in the stomach. I've fought it—believe me, I've fought it! After that day in the pool when I held you in my arms, felt your body against mine, I was determined that I wasn't going to give way again. I've done some lousy things in my time, but I just couldn't take advantage of an innocent, inexperienced, trusting girl, so I forced myself—somehow—to be cold, hard—keep you literally at arm's length.'

Cam listening in a bewildered daze, could say nothing.

'I held out for as long as I could, but then,' he grimaced, 'I just couldn't keep away from you any longer. That afternoon cleaning the tapestries, and then that day at the falls—that's when I really began to be afraid. I forced myself to stay away all the next day, but then, when you came down to dinner and I saw that lovely dress—or rather,' he gave her a wry smile, 'that lovely body in that dress—well, I was just intensely grateful for the New York trip.'

'You really did have to go, did you?'

'I hadn't planned on going up until the weekend, but I decided there and then to make a run for it.' His eyes held the faintest of smiles. 'Even then, I almost asked you to come with me—I had it all sewn up neatly in my mind. It would be a break for you—you've never been to the States and you could pound round the museums and galleries to your heart's content. But of course, all the time,' his voice took on a self-mocking note, 'while I was making such elaborate, philanthropic plans for your happiness, at the same time my subconscious was busy making parallel plans how, once I got you there, away from Tamarind, it would be much easier, somehow, to——'

He stopped abruptly, and Cam prompted huskily, 'To——?'

He pulled a face. 'Why—to lure you into my bed, of course. It's what I've been aching for, ever since I kissed you in the pool. But then, that day at the beach, when I chased you up the falls and you looked at me, the water drops glistening on your face and hair, I knew that—more than with any other woman I've ever known

—I wanted to feel you melt into my arms, to make you as hungry for my body as I was for yours.'

She was dreaming, she must be. A few moments and she would wake, the pale moonlight, the white starry pinpoints of blossom, the heady scent of the orchids just a fading, delectable memory. And yet, there was nothing dreamlike about Matt; his hands, which curved around her elbows to hold her slightly away from him, were warm, real.

Inside her, she felt rising a most extraordinary sensation, a suffocating tenderness mingled with a desire that left her dizzy and helpless. Regrets—regrets were for another time in another existence, the cold light of day, or some future moonlit night when Matt would not be there. But for tonight—a hundred times she had asked herself what it must be like to be made love to by Matt, to surrender herself to his body, her inhibitions all swept away by his physical passion.

Now—she lifted her hand to caress his cheek, and gave him a tremulous smile. Matt, with a smothered exclamation, seized on her hand and pressed his lips to it, before turning it over to drop soft kisses across the palm, so that Cam shivered deliciously. Then, very gently, he drew her unresistingly to him, until she could feel his warm breath on her lips, and kissed her, softly at first; then, as her lips opened under his in almost unconscious invitation, the kiss hardened, his tongue probing her mouth as though seeking some kind of fulfilment.

But then, next moment, he had drawn back, pushing her roughly from him. 'No!' His voice was harsh. 'I swore a dozen times on the flight that I'd still not take advantage of you—and I won't. At least, not yet.' He gave her a shaky grin. 'I promise you, I'll take every advantage of you, just as soon as that ring's on your finger.'

'That ring?' Cam stared at him stupidly. 'You mean—you——?' She broke off, her mind lost in an uncomprehending daze.

Matt tilted her head and looked searchingly down at her. He gave a mirthless laugh. 'Oh, lord, she thinks I want to make her my mistress—as dear old Uncle Matt no doubt would have done! So that's the reward I get for doing my very best to behave like your perfect English gentleman. Oh, Cam, you utter little fool.' His fingers tightened on her arms and he shook her. 'You haven't been listening to a word I've said, have you? I love you, I worship you, I'm totally, utterly besotted with you. Can even *you* understand? I want to marry you.'

Marry? Cam's bemused mind struggled to make credible the incredible. Matt wanted to marry her. How could he possibly? True, he was obviously physically drawn to her—he had made that clear enough, and the new Cam which was slowly emerging like a liberated butterfly from a dried-up chrysalis could now accept, even joyously welcome that. But for him—this sophisticated, self-assured man—actually to wish to commit himself to someone so diametrically unlike him in every way?

'But——'

'But what?' Matt's voice was taut.

'Well,' she said, still quite incapable of making an adequate response, 'we're—we're so different.'

Matt laughed softly. 'Is that all? You know what they say—like repels, opposites attract.' He took her hand and began gently stroking his thumb across it. 'Anyway, that's no sort of an answer.' His voice was light enough, but Cam, whose senses were honed to the nth degree where Matt was concerned, felt the tension beneath the apparent casualness. 'But before you do give me your answer, maybe you should see this.'

As Cam stared at him wonderingly, he bent and picked up the book that he had thrown down earlier.

'I brought you this from New York—a kind of peace offering, I guess, but maybe you should look at it now.'

She took the book from him and it fell open in her hands, so that in the clear white moonlight she saw that it was a volume of photographs, all in monochrome, the harsh black and white totally in keeping with the subject—war.

Rather puzzled, she politely flipped through the pages, until she came to a series of scenes of an ambush; armed men crouching behind boulders, then the vicious fight with and final destruction of a convoy of enemy lorries and their crews on a narrow track above a mountain gorge. The photographer had obviously gone in shoulder to shoulder with the guerillas, trusting implicitly in their ability to defend him as he took shot after shot.

Even in the half-light, the pictures were horrifying, and yet, with her own innate artistic sense, Cam could only admire the extraordinary technique of the photographer, which had made every scene, even those taken under the most hurried, dangerous circumstances, a perfect composition. And alongside the artistry there was something else much more profound, a sense of pity and horror, an intense feeling for his fellow humans, which moved her deeply.

She looked up at him and saw that he was watching her intently.

'They're—they're marvellous. But why——'

In response, he took the book from her and turned back to the title page, where the name of the photographer, in large, bold print, leapt out at her:

M.J. Corrigan.

'You're M.J. Corrigan?' Cam spoke very slowly, her astonishment almost robbing her of speech.

It was a question as much as a statement, and Matt nodded.

'But—but you're the most famous photographer in the world,' she said simply.

Matt laughed and gave a self-deprecating shrug. 'Correction—only one of the most famous.'

Cam was still struggling to assimilate Matt's revelation. 'But we had a retrospective exhibition of your work at the museum last year. It was marvellous.' Then she remembered something else and gave a gasp. 'You came—for the opening!'

'Yes, that's right. I stopped over in London *en route* for this assignment.' He gestured towards the book, then paused fractionally. 'I don't remember you—at the reception, I mean.'

'No, I was on leave at the time, but I heard all about it.' There was a barely perceptible note of regret in Cam's voice. If only she had been there, she would have met Matt—known him for a whole year. Oh, come off it, she thought, he wouldn't even have noticed you, an insignificant nonentity from the textiles department, surrounded as he would have been by all those bigwigs and celebrities.

'It was all very—civilised,' he went on in a reminiscent tone. 'Tea in bone china cups, cucumber sandwiches and—what are they called? Oh, yes,' he said, putting on an exaggerated English accent, 'Garibaldi biscuits.'

Cam laughed. 'I know—at school we used to call them squashed fly biscuits.'

He regarded her silently for a moment, with a tender half-smile. 'Mmm, yes, I see what you mean. Anyway, I thought about that afternoon quite often in the months to come.' His voice had taken on a harsher edge and, seeing etched in his face painful memories which she could not even begin to share, she turned back to the book.

'Is this why you've been to New York?'

'Yes, I went up for the launch. You know—publisher's parties, lunches, signing sessions at Macey's.' He pulled a face. 'My agent dragged me up there. Still, at least I took the chance to have some thoroughly unpleasant intensive treatment on my knee, which they assure me has done it good.'

'Oh, that's marvellous,' she exclaimed, but then a chilling thought struck her. 'Does that mean that you'll——'

She broke off, unable to put the thought into words, and continued flipping through the book, until, at the final short series of photographs, her hand stiffened. The helicopter gunship all but filled each frame, until its menace was almost bursting out of the pages as it approached arrow-straight, fast and lethal down the parched valley, little puffs of dust already leaping up from its trail of bullets in an obscene zigzag pattern of death . . .

She tore her eyes from the book. 'Was this when——?' Her voice shook a little.

'Yes.'

'H-how did you escape?'

'Oh, I managed to drag myself into a dried-up ditch just before it made its return run.' Matt sounded supremely uninterested. 'It was my own fault. I'd been ordered not to go off alone. I disobeyed the rules and,' he tapped his knee, 'I've got a permanent reminder.'

'But how did you get away?' she insisted.

'Very ignominiously, I'm afraid. They carried me, plus cameras, through the mountains to the border.

Fortunately, I don't remember much about the journey—apparently, I was raving and light-headed most of the way with fever. A local doctor did a patch-up job and finally the US consul airlifted me out, so that the surgeons could really get stuck into me. Unfortunately, I can remember quite a lot about that.'

Behind the dry tone of his offhand narrative Cam glimpsed momentarily something of the hardships, privations and suffering he had endured, and her throat contracted painfully. She bit her lip, but a sob forced its way up and erupted as a choked little explosion.

'You—you might have been killed,' she whispered huskily, and a tear trickled slowly down her cheek.

Matt leaned over, and with one finger very gently stopped it in mid-flight. 'Don't upset yourself, honey. I promise you I'll take very good care never to be so stupid as to get myself into a situation like that again. But you understand why I'm telling you this now, Cam, before you give me your answer.' The tension had returned to his voice, heightening as he continued, 'Because if you say yes, all this——' he nodded towards the book '—my life-style—comes with me, I'm afraid.'

She stared at him for a fraction of an instant, in her mind's eye seeing past him to all the future times when she would be alone, while Matt roamed the world, seeking out new, ever more perilous assignments. If she begged him, maybe he would be willing to give it all up for her, but she knew she must never do that. Instead, she would somehow bear all the loneliness, the days and nights of anguish when, instinctively, she would know that he was in danger, against the joy of each return.

'All of my life I've been restless, unsettled—and I don't think I'd be able to change, even for you, my sweet. But if I have you, you'll be a fixed point, an anchor,' he seemed to be speaking as much to himself as to her, 'giving me the security I've never had, to take away with me each time I go, and the knowledge that you'll be there when I get back.' He paused, then went on huskily, 'So please, Cam, for heaven's sake, do say something.'

'Yes, Matt, I'll——' she began in a low, unsteady voice, but got no further, for he pulled her to him, almost crushing her in his arms and smothering her hair, her face, her throat with burning kisses. She was melting in his arms but at last, reluctantly, she pulled herself free, and met his loving gaze with the new-born confidence that was blossoming in her. 'Yes, Matt, I'll be your anchor. Wherever you go, I'll be——'

'And where would you like to live? I've got an apartment in New York, and a small house in Nantucket, but you shall live wherever you want to, my darling. I suppose you'd prefer London?'

'Oh, no,' Cam said simply. 'I want to live at Tamarind.'

The words had come unbidden, but as soon as they were spoken she knew with tranquil certainty that they were true. She loved the house, and to live here, maybe—she smiled softly to herself in the darkness—in the future bring up Matt's children here, to have him, another assignment finished, return to her . . .

'I want to live here,' she said firmly, and Matt laughed as he kissed the tip of her nose.

'And so you shall. I've loved Tamarind myself ever since Uncle Matt first brought me here as a——'

Cam gave a start. Matt was still speaking, but she couldn't hear him. In her overwhelming joy, everything but the fact that he loved her had been obliterated . . . Uncle Matt . . . Matt Corrigan . . . and she, *she* was a Forrester. She must tell him now. It would be easy enough. Look, Matt, it's such a coincidence, but you'll never guess who I am . . . So easy, and yet she felt a frisson of unease, as she licked her lips nervously, and began, 'Er, Matt, I've——'

She stopped and Matt prompted her softly, 'Mmm?'

But she could not say the words, not now, and instead found herself asking, 'But has there never been anyone in your life before?'

Matt held her away from him, regarding her with serious eyes, 'Darling, innocent Cam—I'm thirty-four years old and, whether I wanted to or not, I've lived a vastly different life from you. But they meant nothing to me, and no other woman ever will again, I promise, now that I've found you. You're—you're the absolute antithesis of every woman I've ever come across. Maybe I've been unlucky, but until now I've just never encountered anyone so honest, so genuine, so—utterly guileless.' He gave a rueful smile. 'I guess you can blame my childhood, seeing a procession of glamorous but completely unscrupulous harpies taking Uncle Matt for every last cent they could squeeze out of the soft-hearted old fool. And then of course there was——' He broke off abruptly, his mouth tightening.

'And then?' Cam somehow knew that she was encroaching on dangerous territory, but some inner compulsion, some need to know all she could of him, drove her to persist.

He hesitated, then shot her a tight smile. 'Why the hell is it that women are always so damned inquisitive? But OK, if you really want to know the pathetic details. It was when I was about twenty. I was a photographer's assistant in a run-down studio in Brooklyn, with just my ambition and Uncle Matt's promises to recommend me. I was stupid enough to think that she loved me for my pretty face, that she was different from those poisonous bloodsuckers who clustered around him.' His lips twisted. 'I was crazy about her, and I guess that blinded me to the fact that her interest in me dated from when I brought her down here—showed her Tamarind and Halcyon Cay. The trouble was that Uncle Matt gave no sign of dying merely to oblige her, and so in the end she settled, not for promises, promises, but for something more instant, and ran off with the middle-aged owner of a hypermarket chain.'

Just for a moment, through the bitter cynicism, something of the young, vulnerable Matt Corrigan still echoed, but then he went on, 'End of story. But at least I hope it helps to explain—not excuse, but explain—why I've been such a swine to you, especially tonight. It's all true what I said about not wanting to take advantage of you, but it's also true that I've been fighting my feelings for my own selfish sake. I vowed years ago that I was never going to be stupid enough to lay myself open to that kind of treatment again—and I'd succeeded very well—until you came along! I was nearly as angry with you as I was with myself, and I vented that anger on you, my poor, defenceless darling.'

He broke off, staring moodily across the garden, and Cam put her hands behind his head to draw him down to her in a gesture of comfort. His head resting on her shoulder, she gently, rhythmically stroked his dark hair, until at last she felt his tensed body relax. He turned his face to her, then softly slid one hand up to cup her breast, burying his lips in its soft ripeness.

After a few moments, he began to trace the edge of her neckline, then as his hand moved inside her dress, his fingertips burned against her skin. Through her thin, lacy bra, she felt his thumb slowly but insistently caress her breast, encircling it round and round, until he reached the nipple, and they both felt it spring into tautness under his touch.

Cam gave a throaty little sigh of pleasure, but even as her fingers tightened convulsively in his hair Matt's hand was suddenly withdrawn. Breathing hard, he leapt to his feet, dragging her up with him. For one long moment he held her against his taut body, then pushed her roughly away.

'Come on, Cam, back to the house before I'm driven to forget—between the moonlight and that bewitching body of yours—that I'm a perfect gentleman, for the next three days, at least. That's how long it'll take me to get a special licence—and that's how it's going to be. I'm going to marry you, just as soon as it's legally possible.

Only when she was lying in bed a little later did Cam remember, with that same slight twist of unease, that she had not told Matt about her Forrester connections. She stared into the darkness. She *must* tell him, she thought worriedly. Tomorrow, she would say, 'Matt, it's the funniest thing——' She stopped, biting her lip. Suppose he minded, really minded. Suppose he should think that she had deliberately—— Oh, what nonsense, she was surely making a whole range of Everests out of a minuscule molehill. And yet—'I was stupid enough to think that she loved me for my pretty face, that she was different from those poisonous bloodsuckers . . .' Cam flinched and turned over violently in bed.

'Tomorrow,' she said aloud into the night. 'Tomorrow, I'll tell him.'

CHAPTER NINE

BUT next morning, caught up in the whirlwind of preparations for the wedding, no moment ever seemed quite propitious, and at last her resolve slid away to the back of her mind. Besides, she told herself, firmly quelling the last remaining twinges of disquiet, it might be better, after all, to wait to tell Matt at some more appropriate, less hectic time in the future.

In any case, Matt left for St Hilaire straight after breakfast to make the hundred and one arrangements that were necessary, including calling at the British Airways office in Port Charlotte to book her mother's flight in two days' time.

After several fruitless attempts to phone her mother—it was mid-afternoon in London, Cam realised, and she was almost certainly out shopping or at an afternoon bridge party—she gave up and instead settled to write her letter of resignation from the museum. As she typed at the table in Matt's untidy photograph-strewn study, she had the unnerving sensation that it was somebody else altogether who was sitting there, that she was writing on behalf of another Camilla Lucas while she, the new Cam Lucas, was a stranger even to herself.

Just for a moment, as she picked up the pen to add her neat signature, she paused. Writing this letter had brought home to her the finality of what she was doing, cutting herself off irrevocably from her old, secure existence, and launching her into a new, as yet uncharted life as Matt's wife . . . How had it happened, and so quickly, she asked herself, with a kind of fear, that her well-being—no, her entire happiness and reason for living, had become centred on, was totally dependent on this man? Well, however it had come about, her life from now on, for good or bad, was inextricably tangled with his, for without him there would only be a drab, meaningless existence . . . She wrote the signature and sealed the letter.

After lunch, Cam made yet another attempt to contact her mother. In her letters she had explained that the Matt Corrigan who was employing her was not *the* Matt Corrigan, merely his nephew. But she had not even tried to change her mother's views on old Mr Corrigan, and for some reason she had been very reticent also about the new owner of Tamarind. So now, how on earth was her mother going to react when she discovered that her only daughter was marrying into that hated clan? Cam took a deep breath, then began dialling the code for England. In the event, though, the line was so bad and her mother so completely dumbfounded that Cam was able, without more than the faintest of incoherent interruptions, to give the bare, essential facts, including the time of her flight in just two days' time.

She was smiling to herself, picturing her mother already mentally discarding her entire wardrobe and planning her excursion to the West End next morning in search of the most sensational bride's mother's outfit she could run to earth, when a thought struck her.

'Oh, and Mummy,' she said, her voice lowered, 'I haven't told Matt yet about—who I am, so——'

'What's that, darling? I didn't catch——'

Cam's heart skittered as she heard Matt's voice in the hall and, behind her, the door opening.

'It doesn't matter, Mummy,' she said hurriedly. 'See you in two days. Bye.'

She started guiltily as Matt dropped a kiss on her head.

'Well?' He raised a quizzical eyebrow. 'How did she take it?'

'Oh, very well, I think.'

'You think? You mean she wasn't over the moon at the delightful prospect of having me as her son-in-law?'

Cam smiled up at him happily, the faint shadows already dispersing. At the sight of him standing there in his grey suit—after all, as he'd reminded her that morning, he was not only going to visit his lawyer, but also the bishop—her whole insides gave such a leap of blissful joy that she was almost shocked. Still she managed. 'Well, of all the conceited——'

'Hey, watch it. A little more of the obsequious respect due to your husband-to-be, if you don't mind, or——'

'Or what?' Her violet eyes sparkled with mischief.

'Or—this.'

With a lightning-swift movement he pounced, caught her up under the arms and, as she gave a squeal of fright, scooped her bodily off the chair. He pinioned her so tightly that she could not struggle but lay limply in his arms, her eyes inches from his, her hair tumbling in disarray.

Matt smiled down at her in triumph, but then the smile swiftly faded and his eyes darkened into that expression which just a few short weeks previously had filled Cam with such terror. His grip tightened on her so that she could hardly breathe, but then, as she deliberately put her hand up to draw his face down to hers, he abruptly went to set her down on her feet.

When she still sagged against him, he said with a groan, 'Don't, Cam—you're in my charge, under my trust. I just can't keep my hands off you much longer, so don't make it even harder for me.'

'But I don't want you to keep your hands off me.' Cam heard herself say. 'I want you to——'

Matt put his hand over her mouth and thrust her down on to the chair again. 'I've told you, Cam, stop that at once,' he exclaimed roughly, but then, at the expresson on her face, he went on more gently, 'I'm sorry, sweetie, but you just don't realise the power you have over me.' He ran a hand through his hair and shook his head ruefully. 'It's a state of mind I've managed to avoid very happily for years, and now I can't say I altogether like it. Still,' he stooped to retrieve her ribbon, pulled her hair back and retied the ponytail with the tenderness of a woman, then gave her one of his rare, magical smiles, 'I guess I'll just have to get used to it, with you around.'

He dropped into the chair opposite her. 'But now, down to business. I've got the licence, booked your mother's flight, arranged for the vicar of Port Charlotte to come across to conduct the ceremony—there's a small chapel out on the headland that's still used for the occasional service—oh, and Bob Latham says he'll be delighted to give you away.' He looked at her questioningly. 'So that's everything taken care of, I think.'

'Yes, I think so,' she said, almost breathless as she tried to keep up with him. But then she gave a gasp of horror. 'My wedding dress! Whatever shall I do about that?'

He would have to take her across to Port Charlotte—in a resort, there were bound to be shops where she could find a simple white dress. But Matt was grinning at her smugly.

'Now that's where I *can* help. Just wait here,' he commanded.

She watched in silent amazement as he strode out of the door to reappear moments later carrying a large cardboard box, which he tossed into her lap. Wonderingly, she lifted the lid and delved into the white and silver tissue paper, her hands slightly unsteady with the suppressed excitement that she had caught from him.

Inside lay a shimmering mound of silk, the colour of

creamy buttermilk and so fine that it seemed to have no more substance than a spider's web. Very gently, her breath catching in her throat, she lifted it out and then stood up with it, the box tumbling unnoticed from her knees as she held up the dress. Perfectly plain, with a wide, high neckline and floating sleeves, its narrow, soft pleats fell in a rippling cascade to her feet.

'It's a Fortuny—about 1920,' Matt said. 'I hope you like it.'

When she nodded wordlessly, he went on, 'It belonged to an ex-movie queen who's lived on St Hilaire for years. We've been friends ever since she asked for me to do the photographs for her autobiography. She's got quite a collection of old couture dresses.'

'But how on earth did you persuade her to part with it?'

He smiled. 'All part of my irresistible charm. I told her she wouldn't miss this one—and anyway, I made her an offer even she couldn't refuse.'

Cam shuddered inwardly at the thought of how much he must have paid for this once-only dress. 'But you shouldn't have,' she protested. 'I could easily——'

He put his finger to her lips. 'I'm sure you could, but I know just how beautiful you'll look in it—so I got it.'

'Sorry about the bumpy ride, Mrs Lucas,' Matt said over his shoulder, 'but we'll soon be there.'

Cam, wedged between her mother and her luggage in the back of the runabout, mirrored her mother's polite smile, but inwardly her mind was seething with acute apprehension. She had planned on meeting her mother's plane alone, but Matt had insisted on coming with her, assuring her that he would make both boat and buggy rides as sedate as befitted a prospective son-in-law. But this joking reassurance, far from calming Cam's fears, had only heightened her anxiety.

Fortunately, at the airport and then in the speedboat, Mrs Lucas—affected either by the heat or the flight, or possibly a touch overawed by Matt's personality, Cam was not quite sure which—was almost silent. She began, almost imperceptibly, to relax. It was going to be all right. Her mother was not going to innocently betray her Forrester origins before she'd had a chance to warn her. And on top of that, it seemed that she was even graciously prepared to forgive Matt for the heinous sin of being a Corrigan.

When they drew up at Tamarind though, her mother stood, her hands clasped, enraptured at the façade and the sweeping double staircase.

'Oh, darling,' she began, 'it's wonderful—just how I——'

Almost too late, alarm bells screeched in Cam's ears. 'Just how you'd imagined it,' she blurted out.

Mrs Lucas hesitated fractionally, her eyes darting between Cam and Matt, then she smiled and nodded. 'Yes, dear, it's exactly how you described it in your letters.'

The abyss which had suddenly opened at her feet had closed again. For a second, Cam, almost sick with relief, leaned against the stone balustrade, then turned to Matt, who was behind them with the luggage, to find him frowning, his eyes fixed on her with a disturbing, slightly speculative expression in them. But then the expression faded so quickly that she almost convinced herself that she had imagined it.

Indoors, she escorted her mother up to the suite next to hers. They waited in silence until Colette had put down the luggage and she and Miss Poppy had gone, then, as Cam opened her mouth to speak, her mother enveloped her in a sudden, ecstatic hug.

'Oh, my clever, clever darling!' As she kissed her

daughter, Cam drew back sharply.

'What do you mean, Mummy?'

Mrs Lucas gave her a knowing look, which grated on her, then patted her cheek fondly. 'Who's my clever little girl?'

Cam gave a start as, like a body blow, the meaning of her mother's words hit her. 'No—no, Mummy, you don't understand,' she said urgently. 'I never gave Tamarind a thought. I love Matt and——'

'But of course you do, my darling.' Mrs Lucas waved a hand airily. 'He's a very handsome man, after all—and he seems very taken with you. But, well—*Tamarind.*'

Cam, sick at heart, and feeling all the life go out of her, plumped down heavily on the window-sill, watching her mother, dull-eyed, as she went on, 'And I didn't say anything. I realised that you haven't told Matt—and very sensible, too. Don't worry—it shall be our own little secret.'

Cam tried again. 'No, Mummy, you really don't understand,' she said, too loudly, then hastily lowered her voice. 'It's true I haven't told him, but I'm going to.' She hesitated, then on a swift resolution went on more firmly, 'In fact, I intend to tell him this evening.'

Her mother pursed her lips, 'Now, Camilla, you know I wouldn't interfere for the world,' she began emphatically, 'but do ask yourself—is it wise, at least until——'

She paused, and Cam said impatiently, 'Go on. Until?'

Mrs Lucas gave a faint smile and spread her hands deprecatingly. 'Why, until you're safely married, of course.'

Cam gave a gasp of barely suppressed anger and leapt to her feet, then froze as there was a knock at the door and Colette appeared with a tray of tea. Somehow pulling herself together, she said hastily, 'I'll—I'll leave you to enjoy it, Mummy,' and followed the maid out, trying not to hear her mother's warning undertone.

'And remember, darling, do be sensible.'

Stiffly, almost as though she were in a trance, she went down the stairs, her hand dragging across the banister, then half-way down she stood stock-still. Just below her in the hall, Matt was on the phone, his voice raised angrily, his face dangerously flushed. Who on earth had dared to invite his fury, like the wrath of the gods, down on their unfortunate head? Whoever it was, she quailed for them.

'And you can tell that——' Cam winced at the crude expletive '—designer that if he doesn't agree, it'll be the last book of mine he'll work on.' He caught sight of Cam, and went on, slightly more mildly, 'I'll be in touch. What? Oh, soon.'

He put down the receiver and reluctantly she went on down to him. 'Is something wrong?' she asked, almost timidly.

'Oh, nothing,' he said irritably. 'It's just that my publishers—although for how long they'll be my publishers is far from certain—are bringing out an updated version of one of my books and, against my absolute wishes, they're planning on splitting up the most important series of photographs, which will ruin the whole impact. I thought I'd sorted it out when I was up there, but——' He blew out a long breath, then gave her a rueful smile. 'I guess I'm just too much of a perfectionist for my own good—or anybody else's.'

He put his arm across her shoulders. 'Come out into the garden and help me cool off before dinner.'

He gave her a tender flick on her cheek with his finger, but, though Cam answered his smile, she was silent as they walked, one thought hammering over and over in her mind: all that anger, that reaction over something so trivial. And finally her determined, 'Matt, I've got something to tell you,' withered on her lips.

*   *   *

'Oh, darling, you look wonderful. Such a beautiful bride!'
Mrs Lucas's voice wobbled dangerously towards
sentimental tears, and Cam gave her a hasty hug.

'Now do go, Mummy, *please*, or we'll both be late.'

After her mother, resplendent in pink chiffon and
matching straw picture hat, had floated out, Cam, alone
for the first time, turned back to the full-length mirror.
Was it really her, or was a stranger standing there? A
stranger in a long, high-waisted, creamy silk dress, which
stirred around her in the warm draught from the window,
gently emphasising the graceful lines of her body as she
moved, her silky golden hair curving forward on to her
cheeks, then caught in a knot low on her nape.

She heard the soft crunch of tyres on the gravel and,
peeping out, saw her mother climbing into the elderly grey
Rolls-Royce which had materialised from somewhere on
the Cay and which Matt had solemnly assured them had
originally been used by a Maharajah for bagging tigers.

The car moved sedately away down the drive. When it
returned, it would be to take her to be married to Matt.
She moved away from the window and picked up her
bouquet, made like her dainty coronet from tiny cream
orchids, then she caught sight of her face, rather pale and
serious, though her violet eyes were like stars and a secret
smile curved softly round her mouth. She went downstairs
to find Bob Latham, Matt's bluff Yorkshire-born lawyer,
pacing up and down the hall, his normally rosy face pallid
with pre-wedding jitters.

Ever afterwards, Cam would retain a perfectly clear
picture of every part of her wedding day, and yet, at the
time, it was as though each separate image superimposed
itself on the one before . . .

Outside the tiny chapel, hardly bigger than a large
living-room, a little knot of spectators; then inside, to a
fairy-tale transformation scene. Matt had brought her here

the previous morning, and it had seemed, to her, bare, even severe; now though, it had become a bower of sweetly perfumed flowers, for huge curving sprays of orange blossom, frangipani and white jasmine stood in vases everywhere, pink clouds of hibiscus were piled on every window-sill and at each pew-end tall lilies stood, their white, waxed petals curled back like joyful trumpets from their orange, scented stamens . . .

Matt, more handsome than she'd ever seen him, in a lightweight pale grey suit, white shirt and silvery tie, waiting for her at the chancel steps, watching her come towards him, a look in his eyes which made her feel as though she were treading inches deep on some red plush carpet, not a simple rough stone floor, while at his mouth a slight tightness betrayed, to her at least, that he too was not entirely free from nerves . . .

'Dearly beloved, we are gathered together here . . .' Bob Latham, his task complete, sitting down with obvious relief to the quick, 'well done' smile of his plump St Hilairean wife . . .

Matt's voice, rather husky, 'I, Mateo Jaimé, take thee, Camilla Jane, to my wedded wife . . .' The heart-catching beauty of the timeless words flowing through her . . . 'With this ring I thee wed, with my body I thee worship . . .'

In the minute vestry, her mother wiping away the inevitable tears, then, after the signing of the register, the young vicar saying jauntily, 'You may now kiss your bride, Mr Corrigan,' and everybody laughing, as they were meant to do. And Matt, taking her very carefully into his arms, as though she were made of finest English porcelain, to plant a light kiss on her cheek, though the expression in his grey eyes, for her alone, hinted at something very different, a private message which made her cheeks flush a delicate pink and her breath catch unsteadily in her throat . . .

The photographs, taken on the tiny rough-mown lawn beside the church by a friend of Matt's from Port Charlotte . . . The drive back to Tamarind, in slightly constrained silence, not only because of the chauffeur but also, on Cam's part at least, through a sudden, unexpected shyness, as she found herself sitting next to her husband of less than an hour, his knee against hers, his arm brushing against her skin, so that she felt, through the silky material of his jacket, the vibrant warmth of his body . . .

More photographs, the guests ranged on the double staircase at the front of the house; then, the tension of the service broken, the talk and laughter as champagne corks popped before everyone sat down to the wedding breakfast in the cool, panelled dining-room . . . Matt, the perfect, polished host, witty and charming—Cam, seated beside him, eating almost nothing, yet feeling that she could never have enough of feasting her eyes and senses on him.

When finally the meal was over, coffee and liqueurs were served on the terrace, but as the guests went out Matt put a detaining arm round her waist and shot her a conspiratorial grin.

'Go up and change.'

She protested that they couldn't possibly leave yet, but he silenced her with a finger on her lips. 'No arguments—do as you're told.'

When she rejoined him in the hall, having exchanged her beautiful wedding dress for the loose green cotton sundress which he had said she should wear—and which would, after all, be more comfortable on the flight that presumably they were going to catch, than something more stylish—she saw that he had returned to his favourite casual outfit of T-shirt and jeans.

'Right, I've said our farewells—they're getting on very

happily without us.'

He gave her a quick smile, then took her hand and set off, not directly down the drive but across the lawn then through the plantations, almost dragging her as she lagged back in the afternoon heat. The sleek powerboat was rocking gently at the jetty, their two cases stowed at one end. He handed her down after him, and a moment later the engine purred into life.

To her surprise, though, they headed, not for the faint smudge that was St Hilaire, but out into the green-blue waters of the Caribbean. She watched Halcyon Cay gradually fade behind the spreading ostrich fan of the boat's wake, then turned as she felt the boat slacken speed and saw that an island, so tiny that it would have been no more than a punctuation dot on any map, was directly ahead.

In front of them was a reef, the waves breaking over it where the sharp edges snagged the surface. Matt cut the power to minimum, found a gap in the coral and eased them through. The bottom of the boat rasped softly for a few heart-stopping seconds, but almost before he could shoot her a reassuring smile they were on the millpond waters of a small lagoon.

Cam went and stood beside him and he drew her to him, so that she leaned back against his hard body, her hair whipping about his face.

'Come on, you can guide her in,' he invited, then put his hands over hers on the wheel, and she instantly felt his warmth and strength.

They were at the extreme end of the curving half-moon of white sand, and beyond the beach, almost hidden from view among the palms and flowering shrubs, she could glimpse a low white building—their hotel, presumably. She looked up and saw that Matt was watching her, a smile crinkling the corners of his eyes.

'I hope you approve?'

'Oh, Matt, it's beautiful,' she breathed, 'absolutely perfect.'

And yet—her eyes strayed back to the beach, the milky green water rippling soundlessly up the sand. Soundlessly! Yes, that was it. There was no sound anywhere, no bronzed or pink bodies sprawled in the sun or cleaving happily through the clear waters. Just silence. It was almost as though . . .

Matt jumped from the boat, only the slightest stiffness apparent now in his leg, and held his hand out to her. He led her across the sand to the shade of some acacia trees which opened out to a lawn, rather overgrown, and beyond that, the white building she had seen from the sea, its door and tall, shuttered windows almost lost under a green haze of tumbling creepers.

As they approached, a couple of greyish lizards which had been sprawled at their ease on the wooden veranda scuttered away down the steps. They were the only signs of life, and the rustling palm branches overhead the only sound.

'Yes, that's right.' Matt nodded, completely deadpan, as she turned puzzled eyes to him. 'We're alone.'

As she gaped at him, he dug in his jean pocket and handed her a folded paper. Wonderingly, she opened the thick sheet and stared down at it. But it took time for the convoluted legal jargon to unwind itself, and long before she reached the end, Matt, with a hint of impatience, had said, 'Well?'

'But I don't understand,' she said slowly. 'What does it mean?'

'Tch.' Matt shook his head. 'And I told Bob to draw up the document so that even the most simple-minded of young women could understand it.' He took the paper from her and she watched his thin brown fingers refolding it. 'It means, my sweet, that as of three days ago, Paradise Cay, its foreshore and the dwelling place thereon, are owned, wholly and solely, by Mrs Camilla Corrigan.'

'You mean——?' she croaked.

He put up one hand, gently closed her open mouth and gave her a lop-sided smile. 'Happy wedding day, my darling—and welcome to Paradise.'

CHAPTER TEN

MATT threw open the double glass doors and the inner, green-mesh screen, then turned to lean against the jamb, his arms folded, watching her.

'Well, what do you think? If you don't say something soon, I'll begin to wonder whether I shouldn't have taken you to—oh, Acapulco, or somewhere.'

An island? A whole *island*, and she owned it?

'But—it must have cost you a fortune,' she said slowly, still utterly dazed.

'Well,' he said non-committally, 'I did have to get ahead of a developer from the Bahamas who thought he'd got a deal sewn up to cover the whole place with self-catering apartments. But at least you can see why I told you not to bother much with your clothes. We're quite alone, so there's absolutely no need to dress——' he paused fractionally '—for dinner.'

At the undisguised implication behind his words, Cam felt the colour rise to her cheeks and she said hastily, 'Is this why you've kept disappearing these last three days?'

Matt laughed. 'Too right. It was only finalised yesterday afternoon—I tell you, I've never moved so fast in my life. And then I've had to come across here a couple of times—do a bit of tidying up, stock up with food and so on. What with that, and keeping it a secret from everyone but Bob, I was beginning to feel a bit like a demented grasshopper. Still,' he grinned broadly, 'it was worth it, if only to see your face.'

Cam's heart swelled with love and she gave him a rather

misty smile. 'Thank you, Matt, it's the most wonderful present I could ever have.'

'Hey, no tears, please.' He straightened up and dropped a light kiss on her forehead. 'Now, in the best bridegroom tradition, I suppose I'd better carry you over the threshold,' and he swung her up into his arms.

The veranda opened straight into a spacious, high-ceilinged living-room, furnished with deeply upholstered bamboo armchairs and, in an alcove, a glass-topped bamboo dining suite. Cam expected him to put her down here, but instead he walked over to one of the line of doors down one side and shouldered it open.

Inside, the room was almost dark. Matt set her on her feet and opened one of the louvre windows so that the brilliant afternoon light shafted in to reveal a large bedroom. Here, as in the living-room, the wardrobe, chests and dressing-table were of pale gold bamboo. Cam perched on the edge of the wide bed, automatically stroking the dark blue Indian cotton spread, but then, as their eyes met across it, she leapt to her feet again, her heart thumping in slow, heavy beats.

Matt though, seemed unaware of her confusion. He turned away, opening and closing drawers in rapid succession, then said over his shoulder, 'I didn't have time to replace the furniture, I'm afraid, although all the bedding's new. But if you don't fancy the idea of someone else's——'

'Oh, no,' she said quickly. 'Please—I like all this—it's just right. It fits in with the house exactly, if you know what I mean, so I——'

'Stop babbling.' He smiled tenderly.

Matt closed the wardrobe doors and she watched him come across to her. He stood, making no effort to touch her, though at the expression in his grey eyes her whole body shivered softly as though, like a piece of crystal it had been set gently ringing at a touch.

Then, very slowly, keeping his eyes fixed on hers, he lifted his hands and undid the top button of her sundress, his fingers not quite steady as they brushed against her warm skin, then one by one the other buttons until he reached her waist. She stood quite still as he drew the dress down, revealing her breasts, her waist, her slender hips, until finally it lay at her feet. When his hands slid to her white panties, she stiffened, caught in a sudden freezing shyness, and gave a little murmur of protest, but Matt's mouth silenced her into acquiescence.

He stood back, regarding her, and gave her a strange half-smile. 'Venus arising from the waves,' he murmured, and when she looked down she saw that she was standing in the green foam of her discarded dress.

When her eyes went back to Matt, he was no longer smiling. 'Oh, Cam, you're so——' He swept her up into his arms again, crushing her against him, then laid her down on the bed. He dragged off his T-shirt and jeans, revealing to her his own beautiful, muscled body, deeply bronzed apart from the narrow, pale strip that encircled his loins.

Then he was bending towards her, between her and the single open louvre, so that his face was cast into shadow and she was only aware of the male strength of him. For a fleeting second that terrifying dream of her first night in Tamarind came again, the bull head powerful and menacing, but then it was Matt who came out of the shadow to lie beside her.

Very gently, unhurriedly, he began stroking the curve of her shoulder, her waist and thigh. At the butterfly touch of his fingertips little pinpoints prickled under her skin so that she gave a gasp of pure pleasure, and drew him towards her.

'No, honey, please don't,' Matt muttered into her hair.

'I must go slowly—for you.' But when she turned her mouth into his chest and began tracing little spirals with her lips, his urgent, 'No, Cam, don't——' died on a throaty gasp and he moved on to her.

The sharp knife-thrust of pain died almost as she buried her face in his shoulder to stifle the little cry. Then, as he began to move, her body caught the rhythm from his, moving in unison, until Matt groaned, 'Oh, darling—my darling.' His body gave a convulsive shudder and, still cradling her, he lay still.

After a while, he raised his head and gave her a rueful smile. 'I'm sorry, honey, truly sorry. I wanted so much to make it great for you, from the very first.'

Cam stopped his mouth with her hand. 'But it was,' she said with absolute truth. 'It was marvellous.'

She smiled, then lay back, enveloped in his arms, and drifted luxuriously into a half-sleep. After a while though, she became aware that Matt was gently loosening his hold on her and she murmured protestingly. He bent down and brushed a kiss on her cheek.

'Ssh. Go back to sleep. I'll have a shower, then I'll get us something to eat—you must be hungry——'

'Yes, I am, but——'

Through half-closed eyes she lazily watched him go into the bathroom and heard water running. Even though he was only in the next room, she felt a sudden, quite ridiculous sense of desolation. She reached for her sundress, but then left it where it lay and padded after him. She stood watching the water streaming over his bronzed back, then, almost before she knew what she was doing, she had stepped in beside him, clasping her arms around him so that they stood, locked together, the cool water cascading around them.

At last Matt turned off the shower and shook himself, the water flying off his skin as though from the gleaming pelt of a sea animal. He wrapped her in a pink bath sheet, but as he went to turn away Cam caught his hand.

'Don't go,' she said softly.

'But I thought you were hungry.' There was a faint gleam in his eyes.

'So I am,' she said demurely. 'Very hungry.'

He regarded her thoughtfully. 'You know, darling, you are rapidly developing into a shameless young hussy.'

'Well, what do you intend doing about it?' She shot him a sidelong, deliberately provocative look from under her lashes, then gave a squeak as he ripped away the bath sheet. 'No, I didn't mean it,' she gasped, torn between laughter and sheer terror, but it was too late.

He snatched her up and carried her, struggling and kicking, back to the bedroom. He tossed her down on the bed so that the springs reverberated softly, then as she tried to roll off the far side he threw himself down beside her. There was a very short, unequal struggle, then Cam lay, her wrists above her head, caught by one of his hands. His other arm was flung across her thigh, so that she could not move, but could only lie back, helpless and panting for breath.

Matt, whose own breathing infuriatingly was hardly ruffled, took a heavy strand of wet hair in his teeth and lifted it off her face, then slowly lowered his mouth to hers, tracing around the outline of her full lips with his tongue in a slow, erotic saraband, while, as though keeping time, his hips moved against hers in delicately sensual seduction.

The touch of his tongue, the soft brush of his skin on hers, sent tiny electric charges shivering to every nerve-ending. From somewhere deep inside her, a dizzying, spiralling tornado was building, commencing its slow spin, and she felt herself seized by a power so much greater than herself that it was almost terrifying. Something was being unleashed in her that she dared not abandon herself to.

She tore her mouth from his. 'Please, Matt—don't,' she whispered huskily, in an unconscious echo of his own words earlier, but when he lifted his head she saw his grey eyes lit with passion.

'This is how I always want to see you,' he said, his voice catching. 'You're—you're like those girls in the tapestries. Your face, your body——' his gaze travelled slowly, hungrily over her '—all alive—for me.'

He loosened his grip on her wrists and bent his head to her breast, taking up the nipple into the moistness of his mouth so that she gasped with heady pleasure. Suddenly, magically, all her fear had vanished and she began to stroke him, shyly at first, conscious of her inexperience beside his experience, then more confidently, as she became aware of her power over his body, her hand trailing across his flat abdomen, feeling the ridge of muscles beneath the surface tauten under her touch, the sweep of his haunch, hard and strong, where hers was soft, the long line of his thigh with its faint sheen of dark hair.

She felt him tremble, then he rolled over, gathering her to him, one hand behind her hips, raising her up to meet him as she moved with him, her body seeking release from the fierce tide of desire that was flooding through it, rising inside her to a crescendo that was almost unbearable. She pulled him down to her even more tightly and felt him surge into life with all his mingled sweetness and strength, and then the dam inside her burst, the floodwaters hurtling her away with them so that she was just able to gasp out his name before, with a long, shuddering sigh, she collapsed inert into his arms . . .

It was almost dark when she roused, the last vestiges of evening light trickling into the quiet room. Matt was lying beside her, his head on his arm, watching her. He took her hand and held the palm to his lips.

'Oh, Cam,' he gave her a ragged smile, 'I love you so much, it's hell. I'm sure it's not good for me.' The mocking irony could not quite hide the roughness in his voice. 'My insides hurt from loving you—and come to that,' he added, 'so does my shoulder.'

Cam raised herself on her elbow, then gasped as she just made out a deep, perfect double outline of teeth.

'I—I'm sorry.'

Matt pulled her hair gently. 'Don't give it another thought, honey. My prim little kitten has turned into a beautiful tigress, so what are a few friendly bites here and there?' He rolled off the bed, reaching for his jeans. 'Now, before it gets any darker I'll unload the luggage and get the barbecue lit. Steak and rice salad suit you?'

'Mmm, marvellous.'

They smiled at each other, glad all at once to be free of the intensity of emotion between them . . .

After they had eaten, they sat on the veranda sipping the rich red Californian wine which Matt had produced from the small cellar leading off the kitchen. The light from the living-room was filtering softly through the mesh door, the generator behind the house a gentle hum, and, just visible beyond the fringe of palms, the pale sand of the beach and beyond that again the moonlight flickering over the lacy wave caps. Matt put his arm round her shoulders.

'You look sad, love. What is it?'

She snuggled closer to him. 'Oh, nothing. I was just being silly—thinking surely no human being has the right to such perfect happiness. It's—it's tempting fate.'

He rumpled her hair. 'What a superstitious child you are. You were born to be happy—and you will be, always. At least, if I have anything to do with it.' He stood up and pulled her up too, giving her a brief, warm hug. 'Come on, it's been quite a day. Time for bed.'

*   *   *

Next morning, Cam woke early. For a moment, she stared blankly at the unfamiliar room, then joyous recollection flooded back. Gingerly, for Matt's arm, possessive even in sleep, was sprawled across her, she turned towards him. Still sound asleep, he was lying on his side, his dark hair tousled. The long black lashes hid those sardonic grey eyes and this, together with the heavy stubble on his chin and the half-smile on his lips, gave him an endearing if wholly misleading appearance of vulnerability.

The sheet was thrown back and her eyes flickered down to his knee, the scars of that brush with death healing now but still all too evident. An intense feeling of protective love welled up in her, and very gently she slid down the bed. Her fingers delicately traced the ridges of scar tissue and she lowered her head to brush them with her lips. Matt stirred, his eyes opened and he gathered her into his arms.

The days that followed took on a hazy, delicious languor, from the moment when, after breakfast, they swam or lay on the beach, soaking up the sun, until each night the white drapes of the mosquito net contained them in a private set-apart world of their own, where each learnt the power they had over the other and where Matt made love to her as though he could never be sated with her body.

Each day he took a seemingly endless series of photographs—of the island, the sea, but above all of Cam. She was stiff and self-conscious at first, but soon, under his expert guidance, learned to relax as he set her against the glorious variety of backdrops which surrounded them.

Several afternoons, they went fishing out beyond the reef. Matt would set a simple line and leave the boat to drift where it would, while they lay back on the deck, feeling its gentle sway beneath them, until there would be a sudden twitch on the line and he would haul in a snapper or kingfish. As the light began to fade, they would head back to shore, the low sun gilding their skins and Cam almost drunk on sun and sea and love. They would follow their simple meal of grilled fish sprinkled with fresh lemon juice, and salad, with the gold-fleshed mangoes which grew on the tree behind the house, and all the time a universe of stars twinkled overhead.

The final evening, though, Cam insisted that they dine in style. Matt went off down the beach in the direction of a rocky outcrop and came back with a couple of large, ferocious-looking crabs. While he dealt with them—swiftly, he promised—she shut herself in the living-room, set the table with the best china and glasses she could find, and even discovered a whole packet of candles. True, they were the ordinary domestic kind, but standing in a line down the middle of the table, surrounded by heaps of the small yellow blossoms she had found on a tree near the beach, they would do very well, she thought with satisfaction.

All the previous days, she had worn only her sundress or swimsuit—or less. Tonight, though, she showered, washed her hair, then put on for the first time one of the dresses she had bought in Port Charlotte on the way to meet her mother. In soft white Indian muslin, unwaisted and with a drawstring neckline, it was very simple, yet it set off to perfection her tanned body and golden piled-up hair, and when she surveyed herself in the bathroom mirror she saw that there was a new, mysterious bloom on her like that of some lovely ripe fruit.

When she went back to the dining-room, Matt, who had also discarded his favourite shorts for grey trousers and a white short-sleeved shirt, was lighting the candles. He straightened from the last one, the flare of the match illuminating the sudden spark in his eyes when he saw her.

As she seated herself at the table, Matt, with the air of a magician, produced a bottle of champagne, set amid a bed of ice in the washing-up bowl. And for dessert, they peeled and sliced mangoes into glass dishes then poured the remains of the champagne over them.

Long after dinner, they strolled along the beach, their bare feet soundless on the warm, powdery sand, and stood at the very edge of the water so that it creamed around their ankles. Suddenly, Cam gave a gasp and clutched Matt's arm.

'Look—out there!' She pointed to where, just off shore, the inky blue-black water was alive with a shivering, flickering silver, like hoar frost at a frozen midnight.

'Oh, that's phosphorescence,' he said carelessly. 'It happens quite often.'

'But—it's so beautiful,' she breathed, and looked at him, her eyes alight. 'Do let's swim.'

They pulled off their clothes and swam out into the shimmering water, which clung to their limbs and hair, turning them into strange, silvery sea creatures. Matt dived, then a moment later Cam felt his hands grip her ankles and he was tugging her down under the water into his arms, until she wriggled free and they both erupted, gasping, to the surface.

As they waded back through the shallows Cam stumbled, bringing Matt down with her. Instead of getting up, he pulled her down beside him, and she lay quiescent by his side while his gaze took in the whole length of her body, still silver under the moonlight, her wet hair spread mermaid-like around her. Then his eyes, a strange silvery-grey in the reflection of her body, locked with hers.

'Oh, Cam,' his voice broke huskily on her name, 'you are so very beautiful. I want to hold you, possess you for ever and ever.'

His fingers tightened on her arms as he pulled her roughly to him, his lips warm against hers as he kissed the salt from them. Then, with a silent, hungry urgency that was almost shocking, he made love to her as the waters broke gently around their entwined bodies.

The next morning, as they cleaned the house and repacked the boat, a miserable, tight feeling took hold of Cam's throat and chest. It was all over, all the carefree enchantment of the island. Matt had brought her to Paradise, and now—now he was taking her away again.

Matt, a cardboard box in his arms, met her on the veranda. 'You're very quiet.' He glanced at her, then set down the box with a bump and took her gently in his arms, rocking her to and fro as if she were a child. 'What is it, Cam?'

She gave a shaky laugh. 'Oh—I was just wishing for the impossible. That it could have gone on for ever.'

'But it will, my darling, I promise you.' He shook her arm in emphasis. 'Our love is too strong—too special to need Paradise Cay to make it last, but if ever, heaven forbid, you should be unhappy, or lonely or sad, you'll know that the island is here, waiting. And when we're not here, we'll carry it around with us—oh, like some secret treasure that only we two know about. And yes, it'll be a part of us that will last forever.'

CHAPTER ELEVEN

CAM slowly surveyed the long mahogany table, the green candles, their bases swathed in small, elegant pale green orchids, the glittering crystal glasses and crisp white napkins. She smiled. 'Thank you, Miss Poppy—it all looks beautiful.' Though not half as beautiful, she thought, as our dinner table last night, with odd tumblers and candles stuck into saucers, their light glinting on those piled-up heaps of little yellow flowers . . .

The dinner party, which Matt had arranged before the wedding, was to be quite small: the Lathams, a few of his acquaintances from the Cay, whom she had already met, and one last-minute addition—Charles Christie, a near neighbour who had just returned unexpectedly from Europe. '. . . you'll like him, Cam . . . a friend of Uncle Matt's . . . lived here for donkeys' years . . . it was his Rolls we used for the wedding . . . a bit of an old charmer but good fun—he'll be company for your mother . . .'

'Camilla, dear, if I could just have a word——' Her mother, looking rather pale, was hovering in the doorway.

Cam, with a smile to Miss Poppy, went over to her. 'What is it, Mummy? Are you ill? You know, I'm sure you've been spending too long on the beach——'

'Listen,' her mother's voice was urgent. 'I've just found out that——'

She broke off abruptly, looking past her daughter,

and Cam turned to see Matt at the far end of the room. He looked from one to the other, then raised a faintly quizzical eyebrow.

'Is this a private conversation, or can anyone join in?'

Mrs Lucas gave a nervous laugh. 'Of course, Matt. I was just telling Cam how pretty the table looks.'

'Yes, doesn't it? Miss Poppy,' he smiled warmly at the housekeeper, 'you've done us proud. But come on, both of you.' He slipped his arm round Cam's waist. 'The first of the guests are here.'

And with one puzzled, slightly uneasy glance at her mother, Cam allowed herself to be led away . . .

The last guest to arrive was Charles Christie, a silver-haired man of about sixty, almost staggering under the weight of an enormous bouquet which he presented rather coyly to Cam before Matt drew Mrs Lucas forward and introduced her. Charles took her hand and bent over it in an old-fashioned bow, then, as he straightened up, he looked at her closely, frowing in perplexity.

'But surely—we've met before?'

Cam, in the act of handing the bouquet to Colette, froze as she heard her mother say, in a quick, breathless voice, 'Oh, no, I don't think so, unless—have you ever been to London, Mr Christie?'

He nodded reluctantly. 'Many times, but somehow I don't think——' He broke off, and Cam's heart stopped beating for what seemed several eternities before he shrugged. 'Oh well, I must be slipping. My apologies. I pride myself on never forgetting a face—especially a pretty one—but I'm obviously wrong this time.'

Almost sagging with relief, Cam released her breath just as Miss Poppy appeared to usher them through to the dining-room. At the table, under the influence of good food and excellent wine, the conversation flowed easily around her, but Cam, behind the brilliant smile, was thinking feverishly. Charles's sudden remark had shown her the wafer-thin ice under her feet, which might splinter at any time. She was safe for tonight—but for how long? She must tell Matt. For the past week, Paradise Cay had been their whole world, and Tamarind all but forgotten. But now, the memory of what she should already have told him lurched stridently back into her mind.

She looked across the table at him—exchanging swift glances and seeing in his eyes the unspoken message: Just wait, my love, wait until we're alone . . . She flushed and hastily turned back to Bob Latham. How foolish she'd been to worry. Matt loved her—after all, hadn't he spent all of the previous week showing her exactly how much? And tonight, as soon as the guests had gone, she would tell him.

Her mother's tinkling laugh broke into her thoughts, and simultaneously Charles Christie exclaimed, 'Got it!' He slapped his thigh triumphantly. 'I knew I was right—you're little Cissie Forrester!'

The abyss had opened at her feet and she had plunged headlong into it. Everyone else's eyes had turned to Charles; hers swung to Matt. He was frowning, his gaze slowly travelling from Charles to her mother and finally, as though reluctantly, to her, and as his grey eyes at last fell on her she saw, with a sharp twist of fear, that they were darkening from suspicion to certainty.

All the explanations, the well-I-nevers, the laughter, all that was only on the periphery of her mind, as Matt's steel-cold, challenging stare held her—no, *nailed* her to her seat, as though she were a feeble fluttering butterfly caught on a pin.

Dimly, she heard Charles's voice, heavy with nostalgia. '. . . those marvellous parties . . . the gardens of Tamarind alive with lanterns and fairy-lights . . . And you were how old—fourteen, wasn't it?—when your family

—er——' he hesitated, obviously conscious of the circumstances of the Forresters' ignominious departure from the Cay '—left. And you've lived in England ever since? Married, and with a beautiful daughter——'

Cam, her face stiff, barely managed to acknowledge the heavy-handed compliment before unwillingly, like a bird mesmerised by a stalking cat, her eyes went back to Matt. 'And now here you are, both of you, back at Tamarind. Amazing, quite amazing! Don't you think so, Matt?'

'Amazing,' Matt said, in a cool, level voice, but his eyes were still locked with Cam's and the polite, transient smile on his lips did not begin for an instant to thaw their Arctic winter.

Somehow, the meal dragged on, and somehow, with a strength she had not been aware that she possessed, she smiled and talked until at last, out on the veranda, Lu Latham leaned towards her.

'You look very tired, my child.' She took Cam's hand and patted it, and at the simple action her eyes, ridiculously, brimmed with tears.

'Now, now, Lu. You know that's not something you should say to a new bride.' Bob Latham gave Cam a teasing look, but none the less he allowed himself to be prodded firmly on to his feet by his wife and the party began to break up . . .

'I'm quite exhausted. I think I'll go on up to bed, my dears.' And before either of them could respond, Mrs Lucas was away up the stairs, Matt watching her rapidly retreating back with a grimly sardonic expression.

Cam hesitated, running the tip of her tongue around her lips. 'Matt, I——' she began, but he interrupted, his voice silky smooth.

'Go on up, darling. I'll follow.'

Behind them, in the dining-room, she heard the chink of

china and glasses. Of course, down here the servants were still around. Obediently, she went upstairs, but once in the huge master bedroom which she now shared with Matt, she could not settle. She wandered around restlessly, first fingering the beautiful vase of flowers which Miss Poppy had placed on one of the chests, then sitting at the dressing-table, abstractedly picking up, one after the other, Matt's silver-backed brushes, and then taking great pains to set them down again in exactly the same place.

Still Matt did not come. Perhaps he'd gone off on his own, walking in the grounds. He was angry with her, she knew that, and yet, surely when she explained, he would understand—he *must*. She stifled an enormous yawn. Mrs Latham was right—she *was* tired. Perhaps she would get ready for bed. She put her hands on the drawstring of her pink muslin dress, easing the neckline open so that the faint, golden swell of her breasts was visible, then stopped as she glimpsed herself in the mirror. Surely he would not still be angry, not after all that they had shared these past few days? At the memories she flushed, and then, as she gazed at her dreamy-eyed self, found herself smiling sensuously.

'Rehearsing another seduction?'

Matt was reflected in the mirror. He was standing, arms folded, in the doorway, silhouetted against the landing, his expression quite unreadable in the dim light of the bedside lamps. He closed the door, then came and stood just behind her, looking down at her. He was very pale and as his eyes took in the full curve of her breasts his lips twisted, though whether in anger or pain she could not be sure. In the mirror, she stared up at him, her eyes widening.

'Don't look at me with those damned eyes of yours. It worked once, but I swear it won't work again.'

His voice was quiet, dangerously so. She would have preferred him to shout and rail at her, she thought with a shiver. Her hands, which had been toying mechanically with the tiny silver beads on the drawstring, fell to her lap.

Somehow, she had to break through the hard shell of this cold-eyed stranger to Matt. 'Please, let me explain——' she began, with a break in her voice, and leaping to her feet she put her arms round him. 'You *must* listen to me, darling——' there was a desperate edge to her voice '—I know I was wrong not to tell you, but——'

Matt thrust his hand across her mouth. 'Shut up,' he said, with a suppressed fury that shook her. 'No more lies.'

He seized a handful of hair and wrenched her head back so that they were looking directly into each other's eyes, hers filling with tears from the pain, and blue-black with desolation, his the grey steel of pitiless contempt. For several seconds he regarded her dispassionately, then his lips twisted and he thrust her away from him, so that she stumbled blindly against the dressing-stool and sank down on to it.

Matt shrugged off his jacket and hurled it across the nearest chair, then with one impatient gesture dragged off his tie. Still without looking at her, he said, 'I suppose you and your mother cooked this up between you. Oh, I don't doubt, having met her, that hers was the guiding hand——' Cam tried to protest but he ignored her '—but you—*you* were the more than willing tethered goat, staked out for the tiger. And this particular tiger walked open-eyed into your trap.'

The searing anger seemed to be directed as much against himself as her. 'I suppose I can't altogether blame you. Your mother has no doubt been feeding you with the poison ever since you can remember, and then my letter must have seemed like a gift from the gods.' He broke off momentarily and his lips curled in a mirthless smile. 'It must have been quite a shock for you when you discovered that it wasn't Uncle Matt you had to deal with—he wouldn't have been the first seventy-year-old to have his head turned by a pretty face—but—in the new situation—you played your part to perfection. I should really congratulate you, my dear, on your performance, but you'll forgive me if I don't.'

Cam moved restlessly on the stool, but the remorseless voice went on, holding her there as though by physical force. 'It must have been quite a shock for your mother when she discovered that Charles Christie was to be among the guests tonight. And of course she nearly blew it when she first arrived at Tamarind, didn't she? She couldn't quite hide her triumph, but clever little Cam stopped her just in time, didn't you, my darling?'

'Yes, but I was going to tell you—truly I was.'

'Why didn't you, then? There was nothing to stop you.'

'I—I was afraid of how you would react—that you'd be the way you are now. I've seen your anger—how you were about those dyes—but I'd made up my mind to tell you the night before the wedding. But you were so furious about that book that I just couldn't bring myself to. It—it seemed better to wait for a better time.'

'Yes, a better time—like when you were married and safely installed in Tamarind. Oh, how you must have laughed secretly when I actually asked you where you wanted to live. As if there could be anywhere else!'

Cam shook her head, trying desperately to clear her brain. How could she convince Matt that he was wrong, that in his unreasoning anger he was warping, twisting everything?

'It's true that I love Tamarind—but, Matt, I wouldn't care where I lived so long as I was with you.'

His laugh was a sneer. 'What a romantic, beautiful thought. It's such a pity that I can't believe you.'

His tone stung her, and from somewhere, she salvaged

a few tattered remnants of pride. 'That's your privilege, Matt,' she said, with quiet dignity, 'but it happens to be true.'

But he seemed quite impervious to her words. 'Just one more thing.'

He turned on his heel, strode to the far wall and snatched down a blue-green seascape that hung there, to reveal a small wall safe. Impatiently, he flicked the combination lock, opened it and drew out an object wrapped carefully in a linen cloth.

'Here.' He thrust the package at her. Then, as she stared up at him, he added harshly, 'Open it, will you?'

With trembling hands, she undid the wrapping, to reveal a small statuette of—yes, surely it was gold, and from the exhibits in her museum she realised instantly that it was a Mexican pre-Colombian figure. It represented some pagan god—no kindly father-figure, but a grotesque, fearful creature with something of the terror that its maker had no doubt felt centuries before still clinging to it.

Cam shuddered and held it out to him. 'I-I don't want it,' she stammered. 'It's h-horrible.'

He gave a derisory laugh. 'Maybe it offends your delicate sensibilities, but it will no doubt interest you, my dear, when I tell you that it is almost certainly unique, and certainly priceless. It's been handed down in my mother's family for a dozen generations, and it's what your grandfather wanted so much that he was prepared to risk everything to get it. Well, you've won it all back—what did I say just a week ago, "With all my wordly goods I thee endow"?—so you may as well have this to add to your trophies.'

He broke off, and a jagged smile momentarily crossed his features. 'It's rather appropriate, really, as I'm sure you'll agree.'

Cam forced herself to look at the figure again. It seemed to be some sort of war god, for in one hand it was brandishing a short dagger with its blade covered in gouts of blood, while round its waist was a wide belt from which hung—she saw, with fascinated horror, a row of human hearts, so vivid that they almost seemed to pulsate with the life which had so recently been torn from them.

Repelled, her eyes went to the feathered head-dress, but the face beneath it was so horrifying, its jade eyes staring out at her in blind bloodlust. The lean, hawkish face and the thin lips, twisted in a cruel line . . . Cam jerked her eyes away, only to meet, sickeningly, its mirror image in Matt's dark, narrow features.

Desperate to escape from the expression she saw there, she looked back at the figure. So this was what her grandfather had wanted—coveted so much; this it was that, all those years ago, had set in motion the train of events that was meeting its dreadful climax here . . .

Lost in her own tortured thoughts, she realised that Matt was speaking, almost as though to himself. 'Like a fool, I thought—I really believed that you—so honest, so guileless—were different from any other woman I'd ever met. But no—you were just more cunning, more subtle—and a thousand times more successful.' His voice shook and Cam longed desperately to leap up and hold him in her arms, but the burning scorn in his eyes, the rigid lines of his face, as though he were only holding himself in control by a supreme effort, checked the tiny, impulsive movement even as it began.

'Oh, Cam, I loved you so much, I believed only death could end it.'

At the world of bleak desolation in his voice, Cam's insides twisted with a spasm of anguish. But then the full meaning of his words hit her. I loved you—*loved*. The word rang in her brain like a death sentence, a knell.

'But I love you, Matt.' The words burst from her in a despairing plea.

'Oh, of course, my sweet,' he said with cold, flaying sarcasm. 'It's just that you happen to love Tamarind so much more.'

He picked up his jacket and walked towards the door.

'W-where are you going?' she whispered.

'To my dressing-room.' Then, as she stared at him, he added impatiently, 'Don't worry, I shan't disturb you again—there's a bed there. After all, you've got what you wanted—Tamarind. You must excuse me if I choose no longer to be included, like one of the fittings, in the package deal.'

The door closed softly behind him. With all her senses strained almost to cracking point, Cam somehow felt him standing quite still on the far side of the door, and then, finally, she heard his retreating footsteps and another door open and close.

She realised that she was staring at herself in the mirror again, her eyes huge and wild, like some demented creature. She hastily leapt to her feet and, with the clumsy, disjointed movements of a sleep-walker, undressed. Then, leaving the bedside light on, for she could not bear to have darkness around her as well as within her, she lay down on the bed, waiting for the sleep which did not come . . .

The next few days were, for Cam, endless stretches of empty dreariness to be endured and somehow got through. Matt avoided her at all times except at meals, when he wore a polite, formal, but utterly indifferent mask, and after that single, appalling quarrel, not another word was said on the subject. Although the reality lay between them like an invisible unsheathed sword.

Every night, he would, without a word, retire to the small dressing-room, leaving her to stare for sleepless hours at the pattern made by the moonlight as it filtered through the closed shutters. Time and time again she went over that night, bitterly regretting, now that it was too late, her weakness and cowardice in not confiding the truth to Matt. Quite unintentionally, she had woven a fragile web of deceit, and now it had tightened around them both like bands of steel.

Sometimes, when she eventually fell into a light sleep, she would rouse and turn towards the warm shelter of Matt's body, but then, feeling the bed cold and empty, remembrance would flood back and she would once more lie gazing at that moonlit pattern, her whole body racked with a terrible, aching hunger for him.

Apart from her own despair, Cam was terrified of how Matt would react towards her mother, for he clearly coupled them together as conspirators in his mind. In the event, though, he was formally, though icily correct. He made absolutely no mention of the revelations, and Mrs Lucas, grateful for what she chose to interpret as his tact, was silent too. In any case, her time was becoming increasingly taken up with Charles Christie. He would call each morning and take her off on some fresh excursion or beach picnic, and Cam, furtively watching her mother with dull, lifeless eyes, saw that she was becoming prettier and more youthful by the day.

One afternoon, as she was passing through the hall, the phone rang and she lifted it, only to hear Matt's voice on his study extension. But as she went to replace it with nervous haste, she heard him say, 'Yes, well, it sounds an attractive proposition—it's an area I haven't covered yet. What? Oh, the leg's fine now, so there's nothing to stop me. I'll think it over and ring you back in a few days.'

So Matt would almost certainly be off again soon—no doubt grateful to become involved in some new assignment, for after all, as he had so clearly implied, there was nothing to keep him here at Tamarind now.

For her part, as her only hope of salvation she turned back once more to the tapestries. One evening on Paradise Cay, as they sat on the veranda after their meal, Matt had said that in spite of her resignation from the museum he wanted her to continue her work on them. 'I just wouldn't entrust them to anyone but you . . .'

Now, though, the warm glow of pride she had felt at his words had been burned out into cold, dead ashes, and even though, shut away in that silent room, she worked as conscientiously as ever—in fact, more so, with a feeling that through this she might somehow assuage her grief—she did it quite mechanically. After several more attempts, she succeeded in capturing exactly the delicate pink of the wild rose head-dress, but this minor triumph gave her no pleasure because she could not share her success with Matt.

One morning, she was working on those same roses, Europa's face spread across her lap, when with cruel suddenness, before she could even brace herself against them, Matt's words came flooding back: 'You're—you're like those girls in the tapestries. Your face, your body, all alive—for me . . .'

A shuddering sob was rising in her, when she heard a footstep in the passage outside. He was coming to her—he too could not withstand this separation any more. Her face radiant, she was already scrambling to her feet when her mother came in.

'Oh, so here you are, darling. I've just looked in to say goodbye.'

'Goodbye?' Cam gazed up at her stupidly.

'Yes, I'm off to stay with Charles for a few days. Surely you remember—I told you yesterday?' Mrs Lucas looked at her closely. 'You're all right, aren't you, darling? You're very pale.'

'Oh—yes, yes. It's just——' Cam lied wildly '—I've just pricked my finger rather badly.'

Her mother hesitated, then said, 'Look, Camilla, I know you so much enjoy your work, but you really mustn't spend all your time locked away in here, you know. For one thing, it just isn't fair to Matt. I don't think he's a man to take kindly to being neglected, and after all, you've been married for less than three weeks. Why, your marriage has hardly begun!'

Hardly begun? A crazy laugh welled up inside Cam and she jammed her hands hard into her overall pockets to quell the desperate desire to throw herself into her mother's arms and sob out the truth—that it was over, and the golden paradise which she and Matt had so briefly shared was changed for ever into a barren wilderness . . .

A car horn hooted and outside they found Charles and Matt.

'Dirty weather, my boy.' Charles gestured towards a line of low, grey clouds building out on the far horizon. 'You mark my words——'

'But, Charles, the latest forecast puts it as missing us by miles.'

'Well, all I know is, the last time I saw my barometer drop so fast——'

Of course. They were talking about the hurricane which was prowling around the eastern Caribbean. It had been the sole topic of conversation on the Cay for days, with regular radio reports tracking its wayward path, but all the nervous speculation over whether it would or would not hit them had hardly penetrated her numb lethargy.

Charles was shaking his head obstinately. 'Well, it'll certainly give us a blow before it's finished. I knocked down all my coconuts this morning—don't want them flying around like cannon balls. Did I ever tell you about that time I was up in Jamaica?'

His voice rolled on, but Cam was scarcely aware of it. She was only conscious that Matt, acting yet again the perfect host and husband, had moved close beside her and was standing, one arm flung lovingly around her shoulders, his bare leg so close that the fine hairs on it brushed softly against hers. No one else though could sense the cold unresponsiveness of his body against hers, feel the hard warning grip of his hand on her upper arm as she made to flinch away.

The car moved off down the drive, and almost before it was out of sight Matt had abruptly dropped his arm and turned away from her. Cam tried to speak, but only a strangled croak emerged. He stopped.

'What?' He looked at her as though he hardly knew her.

'I—that is, do you think that Charles is right?'

'About the hurricane? No, he's an old woman. It's heading due east, so there's no need for you to worry.' His voice held that icy politeness which was worse, far worse, than a physical blow, and he turned away again.

But whatever the cost she had to detain him, keep him with her for a little longer.

'Matt.'

He paused half-way up the steps and reluctantly turned back to face her.

'What?'

His tone was not in the least encouraging but, having begun, she forced herself to persevere. 'I was just wondering what you're doing today.'

'I'm going across to St Hilaire.' He was already beginning to turn away again, and she sensed his impatience to be gone from her.

'I—can I come with you?'

He gave her a cool, considering look. 'No,' he said finally. 'I don't think there'd be much point, do you? I'm sure you'll be much happier working on your tapestries.'

When he had gone, she leaned against the stone balustrade, one toe compulsively scuffing gravel into neat little mounds, until she roused herself at last to go back to work. Outside the tapestry salon though, she stopped dead, her hand on the knob, all at once feeling an overpowering aversion to going back into the room. But, if her love for her work was being killed, what else would there be for her in life?

She leaned against the wall as she was gripped by black, despairing misery, so powerful that it almost seemed to crush her in its talons. She simply couldn't go on in this half-life any longer. With barely a word in her defence, she had meekly allowed Matt to judge, condemn—and all but execute her. Somehow, though, she had to break through the totally unjust wall of suspicion and bitterness which he had erected between them. *Somehow*—she didn't know how—she must, she would make him understand the truth, and—she set her soft mouth in a firm, determined line—whatever it cost her, she would do it now, while her resolve was white-hot.

CHAPTER TWELVE

FIRST, though, to boost her confidence she would quickly change out of her dusty old overall. She flew upstairs, but then stopped dead in the bedroom doorway. Matt was standing over by the window, gazing out at the scudding clouds; there was a half-empty glass in his hand and an open bottle of the light island rum on the window-sill. He must have been aware of her, but that forbidding back did not turn and he continued to stare out at the dark sky.

She wanted to retreat, to slink silently away, but she fought down the impulse. This moment, she knew, was a crisis point. To withdraw now, without a word, would only widen the gulf that lay between them, might even make it unbridgeable for ever. She must attempt to cross the gulf, for both their sakes, before it was too late.

She drew a deep, steadying breath and walked over to him. At first, no words would come, so instead she put her hand on his arm and felt, very faintly, a tremor run through it.

'Matt,' she began softly, then stopped as he swung round. Just for an instant she glimpsed the naked pain in his bleak, grey eyes, but then the iron shutters were down and he returned her pleading look with such chill hostility that she quailed inwardly. But then, taking hold of the last oozing remnants of courage, she raised herself on tiptoe and, as he stood rigid, gently kissed his mouth.

As she drew back she felt his whole body give a violent shudder, as though his rigorous self-control was cracking apart, then he put down the glass, spilling most of the contents, and reached for her, pulling her roughly towards him with one hand, while the other caught at the fastenings on the front of her overall and wrenched it apart. He dragged it off her shoulders, the buttons flying in all directions, and she heard him draw in his breath sharply as the full curves of her bare breasts were exposed. Then he pulled her free of it, leaving her only her tiny pink panties.

On Paradise Cay she had gloried in her nakedness, offering it as a kind of gift to his love and homage . . . *With my body I thee worship* . . . But this was different. Now there was no tenderness in his face; it was flushed, contorted with a naked sexual wanting which terrified her.

As he tore off her panties and lifted her into his arms, she struggled against him. 'Please, Matt—*no*—n-not like this—not hating me!' But, unheeding, he threw her down on to the bed.

'Please—no,' she cried again, as he bent towards her. 'Someone—someone may come in.'

Without a word he straightened, went over to the door and locked it. He closed the shutters, so that only a single shaft of light entered, then came back to the bed, his hand already on the buckle of his denim shorts.

As he leaned over her again, the terrifying vision of the bull god from the tapestry and her dream returned once more, but this time, unlike on that first honeymoon night, the vision did not fade. It was here, in the room, with her and she could not break free. Raw, primitive panic twisted inside her and she tried to leap from the bed, but too late. Matt was beside her, and his hands and his mouth were plundering the soft flesh of her body as though he were trying to punish her—or them both—for some dreadful crime.

But gradually her struggles weakened as she found herself melting in the flames of his passion. There was no subtlety, no finesse in his lovemaking as silently, the only sound their breathing, with concentrated purpose, he moved over her body. Lifting her hips towards him, he thrust against and into the yielding satin of her flesh.

As her body caught his rising momentum, her last coherent thought was that never, in all the lovemaking of their honeymoon, had he roused such feelings as he was now engendering in her, physical feelings of such savage intensity that all her being was slowly fusing into one overwhelming need to assuage itself with his body.

Their rhythm, spiralling in a crescendo, was keeping time in her head with the refrain, over and over, Now he'll surely believe me, surely love me again. Someone—could it be her?—cried out, then she felt her womb contract upon itself in a sudden, violent spasm, a shudder simultaneously ran through both their sweat-soaked bodies and, utterly spent, they lay together . . .

Matt's arm, which had been lying inert across her, was suddenly withdrawn. Cam rolled away and looked up at him, a tremulous smile hovering around her lips, but then the smile faded abruptly as she saw his face. He was lying on his side, his eyes fixed on her with a brooding intensity which made her heart judder with alarm.

But she didn't understand. He too should be smiling, relaxed into tenderness by what they had just shared. Instead, though, in the half-darkness his eyes had a diamond-hard brilliance and the lines of his thin, dark face were surely more hard-etched than ever? But perhaps it was only that he, like her, had found it a totally shattering experience, that he too felt as though he had been wrenched apart and remade in a wholly new form.

She put up a tentative hand and caressed his cheek. The

effect was instantaneous. Matt flinched away from her touch—yes, he *had* flinched, she forced herself later to accept—then, chillingly, she saw an expression of such sick disgust in his eyes that even before he moved away her hand was withdrawing itself.

'Don't touch me.' His voice was harsh, the words seeming to be jerked out of him.

Then, next moment, as she stared at him in shocked incomprehension, he had sprung up from the bed and was already dragging on his shorts. Every muscle in her body locked rigid, her eyes tightly closed, Cam lay quite motionless until she heard him go into the bathroom. She heard the shower running, an avalanche of water, as he turned on the taps to full.

He was washing the contamination of her body from himself. As this thought rose in her mind, she screwed up her face as though in pain and put her hand to her mouth in an attempt to stifle the terrible, tearing sob that was ripping its way through her, slowly rising into her throat. But she must not cry here, not where Matt might hear her, and maybe from some faint, lingering vestige of feeling take pity on her. She couldn't bear his pity, she thought fiercely. She couldn't bear anyone's pity, but least of all his.

She rolled across the bed, feeling against her skin the faint residual warmth of his body, soon to be gone as though he had never been there. She curled up on her side, rocking herself to and fro and hugging herself as though she were very cold. Oh, God, what could she do? The whole world lay in tiny, shattered fragments around her in this quiet room, and she didn't know what to do. And there was no one for her to turn to, for Matt didn't want her any more.

Her fingers, which had been plucking restlessly at the edge of the linen pillowcase, stilled suddenly. In the next room, she could hear Matt still moving around. If he came back, she would see again the distaste—no, the *loathing* which had disfigured his face, and she could not endure that.

Quick as thought, she sprang up. Her overall lay in a heap on the floor, but instead she tore her sundress out of the wardrobe and pulled it on, her fingers fumbling with the buttons, then snatched up her sandals. Outside the bedroom she stood still, listening, but there was no sound except the hammering of her own heart. She ran downstairs, almost skimming each step in her desperate haste to be out of the house.

Once outside she tore headlong across the lawns, terrified that she might be seen from the house, and only when she reached the rolling coconut plantation did her feet slow then halt. She leaned up against one of the trunks, welcoming its bristly abrasiveness, and stood with her eyes closed, feeling it sway against her and hearing its heavy green fronds creaking like sails in the wind.

The wind! Only now did her mind begin to register that the normally gentle sea breeze was gusting fiercely around her, swirling in eddies between the tall, stately palms and rustling the hedges of bamboo. Cool against her clammy brow, it gave her a momentary exhilaration, but then the memory of Matt's face lurched back into her mind with sickening clarity.

A desperate need for solitude was growing in her as she wandered restlessly about the plantation. Where could she go? Where could she hide herself to lick her wounds? Not Tamarind, not Hibiscus Lodge, Charles Christie's home—not anywhere on Halcyon Cay, where Matt owned every stick and stone . . . 'If ever, heaven forbid, you should be unhappy, or lonely or sad, you'll know that the island is here, waiting . . .' Paradise Cay! The thought was scarcely formulated when she was off, running breakneck down towards the sea.

Matt's boat was tied up as usual alongside the jetty, but bobbing and bumping against it as the waves hissed around its stern. Just for a moment, Cam hesitated. Matt had shown her how to steer, even indulged her wish to drive it, but he had always been there beside her. Now, he was not. But, just as a wounded animal will try, until its last gasp, to drag itself painfully to a place of refuge, so every fibre in her being was straining her towards that tiny scrap of land where she could nurse her bruised spirit in the isolation she craved.

She scrambled down into the boat, untied it and switched on the power, gently at first, as she had seen Matt do, then gradually increased it as the jetty and the land receded.

Once she had headed out, that same exhilaration swept through her again as she stood at the controls, the wind tearing at her hair and the spray spattering over her face and arms as the boat buffeted through the waves. A crazy desire to shout, laugh and sing, all at the same time, welled up in her, but then, as she finally left the relatively sheltered waters of the Cay, the mad exuberance ebbed rapidly away and she felt the first flicker of unease.

Out here, in open water, the sea was running high, each succeeding wave jarring against the prow so that the boat trembled under her hands. She glanced quickly over her shoulder, wondering for a moment if she should turn back, but the Cay had already vanished under a huge leaden cloud which was now lowering towards her, its dark heaviness matching the sullen greyness of the sea.

For a heart-stopping moment, the boat rolled and lurched as a wave struck it broadside on, and then, ahead of her, she saw the sea uncoiling itself in wave after wave, rising to meet her like some terrifying physical adversary. The wheel slipped under her wet hands and she snatched at

it. If she lost control, if the power failed, she and the boat
would be gone, tossed to their destruction like a fragment
of matchwood.

Just for a moment her grip slackened again. What did it
matter, anyway? If Matt had ceased to care for her, did
she really mind whether she lived or died? But then she
thrust the horrifying thought from her, set her mouth
grimly and struggled to hold her course . . .

She lost all track of time, her only world the surging
waves, the drenching skies and the wind a roaring fury
battling for her mind and body. Finally, she had no
consciousness other than that her hands were somehow
still locked on the wheel, her legs rigid from bracing
themselves against being flung across the deck.

She thought at first that the indistinct grey smudge was
yet another bank of cloud, but then her red, salt-sore eyes
made out first a headland, then a familiar long sweep of
trees running down to the water's edge, and she knew with
silent gratitude that, more by luck than any shred of
navigational ability, she had battled her way to Paradise
Cay.

Even before she had begun to be afraid of the reef she
was over it, the high sea running her across it with only the
faintest judder under her feet. Inside, however, the calm,
unruffled lagoon had changed dramatically into a boiling,
seething cauldron of salty turbulence. Through the driving
rain she made out the small ramshackle jetty where Matt
had tied up, but as she neared it and cut the power the
waves suddenly caught up the boat, swung it round and
wedged it firmly between the beach and the wooden
supports of the jetty.

Oblivious of the rain and wind, Cam leaned her head
down on her arms, letting the tension and the terror drain
slowly from her. At last she roused herself to look at her
watch. But that was impossible! Less than an hour ago,

she'd still been at Tamarind. She shook her befuddled head—surely, she'd been out on these turbulent waters for hours?

Outside the reef, a white streak of lightning leaped into the sea and she heard the rumble of thunder. When she looked up, she saw that the last remnant of sunlight over her head was dying to a faint yellow smear, like the glow of a street-lamp through dense fog. Those huge, threatening clouds must have followed her all the way from Halcyon Cay.

For some reason, this seemed funny, and Cam heard herself giggle, a thin, shrill sound against the wind. Then her legs buckled under her and she was sitting on the deck, still laughing helplessly. Even as she put a hand to her mouth to try to stifle the giggles another lightning flash hit the sea, so close that she seemed to hear it sizzle on impact. She had to get to the house—she would be killed if she stayed here!

Fighting against the terrible weakness which had now spread through all her limbs and which made her want to sprawl there, indolently watching the storm come nearer and nearer, she hauled herself to her feet and flopped down on to the soft sand. Her legs gave way under her again but she grimly forced herself up. Across the beach she stumbled, through the band of palms, their trunks swaying to and fro, among the wildly leaping branches of the acacias, and then at last on to the veranda of the house.

Her cold, wet fingers fumbled for the key, which Matt had casually dropped into a crack in one of the floorboards when they had left. Matt—her face screwed up suddenly, but then she set her lips. She mustn't think of him or of that day—that had been in another lifetime.

As she opened the outer door, the wind snatched it from her hand and sent it crashing back against the wall. An

overpowering smell of mustiness came out at her, but she
dared not attempt to open any of the shutters—they were
already keeping up an incessant clattering which set her
overstretched nerves jangling.

She turned down the switch but the light was a ghostly
yellowish flicker. The generator must be failing. On the
table were the burned-down candles from their last meal
. . . Matt had stood just here, bending over to light the last
one, then as he had looked up and seen her in her new
dress . . . 'Stop it!' she said aloud and slammed her fist
down on the table, so hard that tears of pain sprang to her
eyes.

She lit a candle and went to check the other rooms, but
the roar of the wind, the almost constant flickering of the
lightning through the gaps in the shutters, together with
the thin, darting flame of her candle which fell on sheeted
furniture and ghostly mosquito nets, created an eerie
sensation in her that prickled the hairs in the nape of her
neck.

The impetus which had carried her off the boat and into
the house suddenly failed. She retreated to the living-
room, set down the candle, then huddled into the sofa
cushions and closed her eyes, trying to escape into herself,
away from the fury of the elements. But in her mind there
was no escape—her thoughts were in even greater turmoil
than the storm. Everything had gone—even Paradise had
been destroyed, its blue, gentle sea and sky, this lovely
house, filled with memories of her fleeting joy, become
things of terror.

She lost track of how long she sat there, drowning in her
thoughts, half stupefied by the incessant noise. She roused
to a sudden bang, as one of the outside shutters was torn
free and hurled against the wall. She must try to fix it, or it
would be wrenched off completely, and then the rain and
the wind would be able to get in to her.

As soon as she unfastened the outer doors the wind ripped them from her grip. Somehow she managed to reclose them, then clung to the veranda rail for support, just as the air immediately overhead seemed to splinter under a simultaneous crash of thunder and a jagged streak of pure white lightning. Half blinded, and with the rain streaming down her face, she peered towards the line of trees, her eyes widening in incredulity.

It couldn't be, but surely—*yes*, a figure was sprinting hell for leather across the open space towards the house. Her eyes were still dazzled by that searing flash, and little images danced up and down in front of her eyes, but gradually they resolved themselves into Matt.

CHAPTER THIRTEEN

MATT!

Cam was running across the lawn to him, everything forgotten in her basic human need not to be alone any longer. And yet he was, seemingly, a very angry Matt still. He was yelling something at her, but the wind tore the sound away, while behind them the swaying palms were groaning with a horrible, almost human sound, so she could not make out his words and just shook her head.

He was carrying a box, but he put his other arm round her waist and, almost pulling her off her feet, dragged her up the steps into the house and dumped her roughly on the carpet.

'But the shutter,' she gasped. 'It's torn loose.'

'You stay right here,' he ordered curtly. 'Don't you dare set a foot over the doorstep again.'

He vanished, and after a few moments she heard the shutter banged to and he reappeared. While he struggled to close the door again, she leaned back on the arm of the sofa, feeling her joy at seeing him vaporise into her former black unhappiness and despair. The storm had changed nothing, that was obvious. His face still wore that hard mask, his mouth was still set in that thin line, and when he turned round he hardly seemed to look at her.

'Are you all right?' His voice was brusque.

Cam nodded.

'You little fool—you could have been killed. Do you

172

know that?'

They stared at one another in the greenish half-light that was filtering into the room.

'H-how did you know I was here?'

'I didn't. It was a—fortunate guess.' Still there was no trace of emotion in his voice. 'I went down to the jetty, decided it was too rough to risk it to St Hilaire, then realised the boat had gone. I——' he hesitated, then went on jerkily '—I went back to the house and searched for you. I rang Charles but he hadn't seen you, so I phoned Nick Alvarez—he owns the new marina over in Port Charlotte harbour. He said no boat had come in that morning, and added, just for free, that anyway only a brainless idiot would be out in such weather.

'So then I rang Charles again and somehow he managed, without alarming your mother—she, no doubt, still thinks you're safely tucked up in Tamarind—to meet me on his jetty with the keys of his boat. I've run it up in the lee on some rocks, so I'm hoping it'll be safer there than mine,' his voice took on a dry tone, 'which is at this moment being tossed about on the beach like the driftwood it will no doubt be by morning.'

'Oh, no. I'm sorry——' she began, but he waved a peremptory hand to silence her.

'Think nothing of it. After all, a power-boat is easily replaceable, whereas—whereas——'

From one of the bedrooms, there came a terrifyingly loud crash. Matt put his head round the door, then closed it again quickly.

'Nothing to worry about—just a couple of tiles come through the ceiling.'

'Oh!' she gasped, and for the first time he really seemed to look at her. He came across to her and put his arm across her shoulder. But then, just as quickly, he dropped it as though her skin had burned him, a gesture which sent a sickening chill right through her.

'There's absolutely nothing to be afraid of,' he said, the formality in his tone making her wince. 'The hurricane is well past us now.'

'But you said it wouldn't come at all.'

'And I was right. This is bad enough, but it's just the final nasty tweak in its tail. If you'd really been stupid enough to sail right into the heart of it—well——' he shrugged expressively '—but even so, we can't risk staying up here. Another load of tiles may break loose, or a tree could be blown down across the house.'

She followed him in chastened silence as he took up the candle which she had lit earlier and opened the cellar door.

'Come on,' he said. 'We'll be safe down here.'

Go down into that horrible yawning pit of blackness? Cam, her nerves already stretched almost to breaking point, shuddered and took a step back. 'No, I can't.'

But Matt fastened his free hand like steel round her wrist. 'Yes, you can. OK, I'll go first—then if there are any man-eating spiders they can have me first, but you're coming too.' And he drew her down the steps.

The cellar was small, lined with roughly faced stone, and though the air struck chill it did not seem damp. Along one wall was a wooden wine-rack, while on the other was a low stone shelf on which Matt set down the candle before disappearing back up the steps. He was soon back, though, with a handful of new candles.

'Light these, while I bring down the rest of the stuff.'

He disappeared again, and this time when he returned he had scooped up huge armfuls of bedding and towels. Finally, he fetched the box he had brought with him, then closed the door behind him, and the tumult of the storm was magically all gone. He put down the box, very slowly straightened up and turned to face her. He was so close that she could feel his breath on her cheek, could see her own face in the soft candlelight gleam of his eyes.

She shivered and he took hold of one of her hands. 'You're frozen—chilled right through.' His gaze went from her face to her body, and just for a second something seemed to flicker in his eyes, but when he raised them again they were still fierce. 'That dress—it's soaked. Why the hell didn't you get into something dry?'

Cam, looking down at herself, saw with astonishment that rivulets of water were running down her legs and her sodden dress was clinging horribly to her body. 'I—I didn't think.'

Matt picked up one of the bath towels and unfolded it. 'Get out of your dress and dry yourself on that.' And he turned abruptly away to light the candles.

Cam dropped the towel on the shelf and very slowly—and thoughtfully—slid out of her dress. As she did so, she realised that underneath she was naked—in that far-distant time when she had run headlong out of the house at Halcyon Cay, she had only stopped long enough to pull on the dress.

She picked up the towel, then hesitated, glancing up at Matt. But he seemed to be extremely busy at the far end of the cellar, his back turned towards her with that same uncompromising deliberateness as he had shown in the bedroom at Tamarind.

And yet . . . There was something, some quite intangible sensation emanating from him . . . Was it remotely possible that Matt was not angry with her now—at least, not about her apparent deception, even if he was still seething over her foolish flight into the storm? Even as this tiny flicker of hope stirred within her, she paused. Supposing she approached this unapproachable stranger, wasn't she risking another cold rebuff—or worse? But in the last few hours she seemed to have grown up a great deal. Her grandfather had lost everything on the turn of a card. Could she, with one final gambler's throw of the dice, possibly win back her marriage?

'Matt.'

He turned slowly, but still did not look at her.

'W-will you dry my back, please?'

'No.'

There was a dead bleakness in his face, but she persevered. 'Please,' she said again.

'I've told you—*no*. I've forfeited all right ever to touch you again.'

Even as his words fanned the spark of hope into a burgeoning flame, Cam took the few steps to him then held out the towel and put her other hand on his arm, feeling it as taut as a strung bow.

'Please, Matt—I'm very cold.' She spoke softly, and gave a whole-body shiver that was not altogether counterfeit.

Without further protest he took the towel, and she turned round so that he could rub her with it, gently, almost diffidently at first, and then more briskly, until her back glowed. Then he put down the towel and picked up a sheet from among the mounds of bedding.

'Keep still.' Unsmilingly, he cocooned her in it, his fingers brushing across her skin in the most perfunctory of touches, then he lifted her wet hair from her neck, to wrap it in a dry towel. Somehow he was still keeping himself rigidly in check, and somehow she had to break through his iron control and reach out to him one more time.

His blue denim shorts were almost black and his

white shirt was moulding itself transparently to his chest, so that she could see the faint shadow of dark hair.

'Aren't you going to change, too?'

Before he could answer, she put her hands up to the front of his shirt and very deliberately undid the top button. Under her fingers, she felt his heart flutter then beat a little quicker as she went on to the next. She undid it, then stopped, her fingers spread across his chest, and when she looked up at him she saw that he was watching her, his eyes still wary but with another emotion also flickering in them.

'I didn't lie to you, you know, Matt,' she said softly. 'I fell in love with you, and when I remembered Tamarind, I was afraid to tell you in case you——' a little, sad smile flitted across her face and she went on hastily to the next button '——in case you didn't love me any more.'

'I know.'

Her busy fingers stopped.

'You—know?' she said slowly.

'Yes, I know now—now that it's too late.' His voice broke momentarily, but he forced himself to go on. 'It's only since—since you went off today and I was so afraid—that I'd never see you again, that I finally came to my senses. But now—after this morning——'

'After this morning, when you looked at me with such contempt, as if—as if you hated me?'

His hands reached up to her and he shook her gently. 'All the contempt, all the hatred—it wasn't directed at you, my darling, but at me, for what I'd done to you.' He gave her a bleak, desolate smile. 'So at least you know the truth now—even though everything's over between us.'

The hope that had been building in her faltered. 'Over?'

'Our marriage—it's finished. After the way I behaved——' His mouth tightened in self-disgust. 'I—I practically raped you. You could never forgive that, and I wouldn't expect you to. Oh, Cam, what did I do to you?'

She looked up, seeing the torment and remorse in his grey eyes, and realised with quickening insight that for perhaps the only time in their marriage this tough, hard-edged, *proud* man was wholly vulnerable, wholly in her power. The thought was almost frightening, but she took both his hands in hers and, very slowly they moved towards one another. But still Matt wouldn't allow himself to break, wouldn't take her in his arms, not even when she smiled at him.

What else could she do? Almost without conscious thought, Cam buried her face against his damp chest and gave a loud sob. Instantly, all the tensions, not only of hours but of days and nights, came to a spontaneous head and erupted as more sobs, genuine this time, shook her whole body. She felt his arms go round her, holding her tightly to him.

'Oh, Cam, please stop,' he said in an agonised appeal. 'You know I can't stand it when you cry.' Then finally, '*Please*, darling.'

At last she stopped and Matt held her away from him, softly brushing away the final few tears with his fingertips. Behind his lop-sided smile there was a question in his eyes, and in answer she trapped his hand against her face, dropping light, soft kisses on to the hard palm, then gave him a bewitching smile over it.

'You must change, too.'

And, without waiting for his answer, she opened his shirt and pulled it off. She slid her hands softly down over the flat lines of his stomach to the zip of his shorts, and very slowly, her fingers trembling slightly, undid it.

Then, before he could stop her, she slid to her knees on the ground in front of him to ease first the water-stiffened denim, then the briefs down over the hard lines of his thighs, so that the candlelight gleamed on his damp skin and gave it a sheen like rippling silk.

Very deliberately, she gathered his pale hips to her and gently buried her lips in his inner thigh, feeling the soft, dark hair brush delicately against her cheek. Above her, she heard him give a faint sigh as a tremor shuddered through him, then he too sank to his knees.

For long moments, their breathing totally suspended, or so it seemed to Cam, they stared intently into each other's eyes, then Matt's lips twisted and he said huskily, 'Oh, sweetheart.'

Just behind them was the billowing mound of bedding. He laid her gently in it, as though in a nest of down, then, lying beside her, gathered her into his arms. This time, he made love to her with a gentle, heart-cracking tenderness that made her ache until she almost felt she would break down and cry again; but then, out of that ache grew a deep wanting that melted her very bones and made her tremble softly in his embrace . . .

Afterwards, they lay very still, his dark head pillowed against her breast, his arms still holding her, as though unable to let her go. She gave a tiny sigh of utter, blissful contentment. The storm raged on outside, but in here she was secure, safe in Matt's arms forever . . .

Forever? Memory flooded back. Matt was going away—soon. She'd heard him say so—off on another frightening assignment . . .

He must have felt the quiver run through her body, for he raised his head lazily, then said quickly, 'Darling, don't look like that. What's wrong?'

'I've just remembered. You're going away,' she said unsteadily. 'Oh, it's all right, honestly,' she continued rapidly. 'I promise I won't mind—I won't try and stop you, or anything. I—I heard you on the phone——'

'Sssh.' Matt put a finger to her lips. 'Yes, it's true—they wanted me to go out to the Middle East. But did you also hear me say I'd let them know? Well, I have—and I'm not going.' He pulled a rueful face. 'For years, I've told myself I had some kind of mission in life to show the utter futility of war, but in the end I think it was simply that I was hooked on danger and excitement. Now, well,' he shrugged slightly, as she felt the joyous relief surge through her, 'wars will go on, however hard we try. And besides,' he gave her a smile that made her insides flutter, 'I now have something infinitely more precious in my life than excitement. I'm not giving up photography, but, hand on heart, no more foolhardy risks. In fact, I've already got a project in mind,' there was a gleam of a smile in his eyes which momentarily puzzled her, 'which won't take me far from home, I promise you. So you see, tough-guy, free-wheeling Matt Corrigan has turned into a tame tiger!'

He dropped a kiss on her nose, then uncurled himself and padded over to the far end of the cellar. Cam watched him, a shaft of blissful love transfixing her like an arrow. Matt, a tame tiger? Never in a million years. Restless, moody, temperamental, she would always have to give him the freedom he craved, she knew that. But he always would come back to Tamarind—and to her.

He gave a shout of triumph and turned back to her, holding up a bottle of champagne. 'I thought there was one left! It's not chilled, I'm afraid, and I seem to have forgotten to bring the crystal flutes across with me, but otherwise—perfect.'

He plumped down beside her. 'I hope you don't object to sharing the bottle with me?' He released the cork deftly and supported the bottle while Cam, between her laughter, tried to catch some of the foaming nectar.

'Hey, keep still. You've spilled it.'

Matt lowered the bottle and with his tongue licked the golden trail from her stomach up to her breasts and finally in a warm, sensuous line to the base of her throat.

'Now,' he said softly against that beating pulse. 'I snatched up some food to bring with me. I knew that if—when I found you, we could be stuck wherever you were for days. So, are you hungry?'

Cam's eyes were closed. 'No,' she whispered.

'That's strange. Neither am I. But the storm isn't going to ease for hours, so what can we possibly do to while away the time, I wonder?' His voice was a seductive, husky murmur, his lips wooing her, moving down from her throat to her breast as his hand closed over it possessively.

'I—I really don't know.' She tried to keep her voice totally matter-of-fact, but its throaty tincture betrayed her and she felt him smile against her soft ripeness.

'I'll just have to suggest something, then.'

His arms went round her, and he drew her down with him again into their warm nest . . .

CHAPTER FOURTEEN

'I CAN'T do my tie. Fix it for me, will you?'

Matt appeared in the bedroom doorway just as Cam tucked the last stray golden tendril into her smooth chignon.

As she fidgeted with the tie, he scowled. 'I hate this bloody outfit, and besides, the collar's too tight.' He tugged at it irritably.

'Now stop it,' Cam scolded. 'And stand still.' She gave the black bow-tie a final pat, then put her hands on the snowy expanse of his frilly evening shirt. 'You look lovely.'

Matt grinned down at her repentantly and she felt him relax against her outspread hands. 'Sorry, honey, but I guess I'm—well, a bit uptight tonight.'

He picked up the long rope of pearls which was lying in its silk-lined box on the dressing-table. 'Turn round.'

He doubled the shimmering strand and dropped it over her head, so that the pearls gleamed against her throat, imparting a soft glow to her face. She felt his fingers hooking the clasp, then he bent his head and kissed the nape of her neck, sliding his hands around her waist to hold her close to him.

'Oh, Matt,' she murmured. 'I do wish you hadn't booked this dinner—I'd much rather stay——'

In the hall of the apartment, the phone rang. Matt gave her a final kiss, then went out briefly to answer it.

'The cab's downstairs. Ready?'

Cam, smoothing down the skirt of her plain, black

crêpe dress, looked up and, catching his eye, pulled a rueful face. 'It's a bit tight still.'

He slanted her a meaning look, but only said, 'You know something, Mrs Corrigan? You look great.'

She picked up her paisley cashmere wrap, then hesitated. 'Look, I think I'll just phone——'

Matt raised a reassuring hand to silence her. 'No need. I rang while you were in the bathroom—well, I had plenty of time to kill.' He grinned at her as he ushered her firmly to the door. 'Charles answered. Everything's just fine, although I gather your mother and Miss Poppy were upstairs coming to blows over whose turn it was for the bath.'

Outside the apartment block, the New York evening traffic snarl was still in full spate, and Matt sat in the rear seat of the cab, tapping his fingers impatiently against his knee.

'It would have been a hell of a lot quicker to walk,' he grumbled.

'Not in these shoes.' Cam held up one slim foot, which was encased in a spike-heeled black patent pump.

What *was* the matter with Matt tonight? she asked herself. Irritable, on edge, and yet the whole idea of coming up to New York for a couple of nights to celebrate, if rather belatedly, their first wedding anniversary, had been solely his.

The cab at last crawled to a halt. Matt paid the driver and led her across the pavement towards an open door.

'But, Matt,' Cam looked about her in puzzlement, 'this isn't a restaurant. It's a——'

'Gallery. That's correct.' He put his hand on her back, propelling her suddenly unwilling legs forward.

The crowded, smoke-filled reception room was redolent of luxury, with its off-white shaggy-pile carpet, low, ultra-modern teak furniture and ultra-discreet lighting. As Cam looked about her in total bewilderment, from among the buzz of twenty lively conversations a formidable-looking woman emerged, whom Matt introduced as his agent, Miriam. In her turn, she introduced Cam to a procession of smiling, hand-shaking faces, then someone thrust a glass of chilled white wine and a plate of tiny smoked salmon *bouchées* at her.

'Matt, you really must come and meet——'

He was drawn away from her, and she leaned against the wall, glancing down at the glossy booklet which someone had thrust on her . . . M. J. Corrigan: *Images of Love*, and below it—Cam almost spilt her drink—a head and shoulders photograph of herself. It was the close-up shot that Matt had taken of her that day at the falls—tousle-haired, solemn-faced, but with water drops gleaming on her hair like stars, and in her eyes an unmistakable inner glow.

When, almost fearfully, she glanced round, past all the heads and the grey haze, she realised for the first time that every wall was lined with photographs. With slow deliberation, like a sleep-walker, she began to walk around the room, now almost unaware of the little knots of conversation, the smiles and nudges of recognition. On this wall were shots that Matt had taken on Paradise Cay during their honeymoon: one after another of her, lying on the beach, in the water, in the shade of the acacias, smiling, occasionally serious, yet with a bubbly joy which leapt out at the viewer from the flat monochrome . . .

She moved on, lost now to everything else, and marvelling, not only at the sight of herself in a hundred different poses, but also at the way Matt's genius had made each one a work of art, revealing, more tellingly than words, the changes that a year had wrought in her.

That open, girlish smile, as she tossed her hair back, and yes—Cam blushed faintly—that naked longing; they underwent a subtle change as a bloom of fulfilment settled on her, like a golden glow.

It seemed to her, as she intently studied the final few photographs, that gradually that other Cam drew into herself, a secret smile hovering around her lips, a private joy shining in her like a steadily glowing candle-flame. Here, she was leaning back in a chair on the veranda at Tamarind, asleep, though her hands, even in sleep, curved protectively across her distended abdomen and that secret smile still played around her mouth.

Then, in a shot which Matt had imbued with an almost religious beauty, she was lying back, her sweat-soaked hair still plastered to her forehead as she reached up to take the tiny baby which a pair of hands held out to her. In the final photograph of all, she was back on the veranda and he had captured the moment when, quite oblivious of the camera, she held the contentedly sleeping baby cradled to her, one tiny starfish hand still outspread against her breast.

'Little Matthew's quite photogenic, don't you think?' Matt slipped his arm around her waist. His tone was casual enough, but she sensed the tension behind it. 'You don't mind, do you, darling—about all this, I mean?' His gesture took in all four walls.

'Now, Cam,' Miriam loomed behind them, 'You really must persuade this cussed husband of yours.'

'Persuade him?' Cam was still almost too overwhelmed by emotion to speak.

'I've got a top baby products manufacturer offering the moon for the use of that last shot when the book comes out. Do get to work on him, there's a sweetie.'

When Cam stared at them both uncomprehendingly, Matt said, a shade ruefully, 'I'm afraid I've been

talked into it—releasing the photographs in book form,
I mean. But that's all—I'm not having any
manufacturer using you and Matthew for cheap
publicity.'

'Cheap?' An outraged snort came from Miriam's
direction. 'He calls that sort of money cheap?'

Matt shook a half-joking finger at her. 'Now,
Miriam, you know that the only thing perturbing you is
your ten per cent.'

Even as the indignant retort sprang to Miriam's lips, a
thought flashed into Cam's mind and she put a hand on
his arm. 'Look, Matt, I wouldn't mind, really. And I've
had a marvellous idea—let them have the photograph,
but we'll give the proceeds to that new children's charity
in Port Charlotte that Lu Latham's helping to set up.'

Matt drew her to him and kissed her cheek. 'A great
idea! OK, Miriam, you can go ahead. And now, you'll
have to excuse us—we're leaving. Cam's very tired.'

Once outside, in the warmth of a Manhattan
September evening, Cam stopped. 'I wasn't tired,' she
protested.

'But I am.' He grinned down at her, but then his face
became serious. 'And you really don't mind—about the
exhibition and the book—making our private love
public property?'

'No, honestly, I don't. But why did you do it?'
Puzzlement still showed faintly in her eyes.

He gave her a rather shaky smile. 'Because, my love,'
you've made me happier in the last year than I would
ever have believed possible. And, apart from giving you
the odd bauble,' he touched the pearls with his little
finger, 'this was the only way I could think of to say
thank you, and to shout from the rooftops to the whole
world that I love you, adore you.' And, oblivious of the
curious glances from the crowded pavement, he

snatched hold of her hand and pressed it to his lips.

When he raised his head, though, Cam saw a poignant, intense look in his eyes and she knew that she must lighten his mood.

'The only way?' Her voice was teasing. 'I don't know about that. You've always shown me, very convincingly, how much you love me.' Her eyes shone mischievously. 'Why don't we go home now, instead of going out to dinner? After all, I'm always willing to be convinced all over again.'

Coming soon
to an easy chair near you.

FIRST CLASS is Harlequin's armchair travel plan for the incurably romantic. You'll visit a different dreamy destination every month from January through December without ever packing a bag. No jet lag, no expensive air fares and *no* lost luggage. Just First Class Harlequin Romance reading, featuring exotic settings from Tasmania to Thailand, from Egypt to Australia, and more.

FIRST CLASS romantic excursions guaranteed! Start your world tour in January. Look for the special **FIRST CLASS** destination on selected Harlequin Romance titles—there's a new one every month.

NEXT DESTINATION:
AUSTRALIA

 Harlequin Books

JTR3

They went in through the terrace door. The house was dark, most of the servants were down at the circus, and only Nelbert's hired security guards were in sight. It was child's play for Blackheart to move past them, the work of two seconds to go through the solid lock on the terrace door. And then they were creeping through the darkened house, up the long curving stairs, Ferris fully as noiseless as the more experienced Blackheart.

They stopped on the second floor landing. "What if they have guns?" Ferris mouthed silently.

Blackheart shrugged. "Then duck."

"How reassuring," she responded. Footsteps directly above them signaled that the thieves were on the move, and so should they be.

For more romance, suspense and adventure, read Harlequin Intrigue. Two exciting titles each month, available wherever Harlequin Books are sold.

INTA-1

Harlequin Presents®

Coming Next Month

#1343 A MATTER OF WILL Robyn Donald
Lora has no intention of joining the throng of women who fall for Matt Duncan
like ninepins. After all, she has reason to dislike him even before they meet.
But resisting him proves to be more difficult than she expects...

#1344 HAZARD OF LOVE Sally Heywood
Goldie and Lucas share a deep attraction, but they just can't see a future
together when she's a Hollywood starlet used to a glamorous nomadic
existence, and he's a farmer in a small English village. A farmer looking for the
perfect country wife...

#1345 RITES OF POSSESSION Charlotte Lamb
Christabel is just supposed to take little Nina and Dani to their uncle in
Brittany, then leave for her holidays. Reclusive Roland de Bellème, however,
isn't expecting the girls, and he has other ideas about how far Christobel's
responsibilities should go...

#1346 NO SURRENDER Mary Lyons
Oriel thinks Jake Emmerson is a bad-mannered chauvinist. Jake thinks Oriel is a
dizzy blonde. When they're stranded together in dangerous circumstances in
Syria, they have a chance to revise their opinions!

#1347 NIGHT FIRES Sandra Marton
For Gabrielle, her flower shop in New Orleans is a refuge she badly needs.
And even though James Forrester has rescued her from a nasty accident, her
past won't let her get involved with him. But James is not a man who's
easily deterred...

#1348 TRIAL BY LOVE Susanne McCarthy
Caroline is floored when fellow barrister Matt Farrar-Reid wants to know more
about the woman under the wig and gown. Not until they're away from the
courtroom does she see him in a different light. Then she finds herself facing
an unexpected choice.

#1349 TENDER PURSUIT Jennifer Taylor
Private investigator Martha Clark readily agrees to track down a real-life
gigolo—it should be an intriguing challenge. But when Quinn Maxwell finds out
she's watching him, he nearly turns the tables on her

#1350 JAVA NIGHTS Karen van der Zee
Teaching school in Indonesia is part of Rae's effort to rebuild her life. It offers
its own problems, however, in Anouk, her most uncooperative pupil. But Rae
has even more problems with the girl's attractive but uncompromising father,
Jason Grant.

Available in March wherever paperback books are sold, or through
Harlequin Reader Service:

In the U.S.
P.O. Box 1397
Buffalo, N.Y
14240-1397

In Canada
P.O. Box 603
Fort Erie, Ontario
L2A 5X3